Only one fact stood out in his mind at that moment. He had to learn the riddle of the Duveen letter, and he had to learn it within the next half-hour. Claude understood; the things he wanted to know could wait. Beyond that point, Rupert's thinking was in a turmoil. The events of the last twenty-four hours seemed so irrelevant to his own affairs, so unreal. He had been brave enough in his day, he hadn't won the Military Cross at Monte Cassino for nothing. But all this gun play and secret-agent scenario had been totally unexpected . . .

Also by Edwin Leather:

THE MOZART SCORE
THE VIENNA ELEPHANT

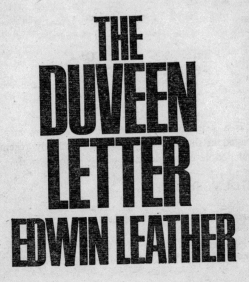

THE DUVEEN LETTER

EDWIN LEATHER

PINNACLE BOOKS   NEW YORK

This is a work of fiction. All the characters and events portrayed in this book are fictional, and any resemblance to real people or incidents is purely coincidental.

THE DUVEEN LETTER

Copyright © 1980 by Edwin Leather

A Pinnacle Books edition, published by arrangement with Doubleday & Company, Inc.

First printing, November 1981

ISBN: 0-523-41542-7

Cover illustration by David Mann

Printed in the United States of America

PINNACLE BOOKS, INC.
1430 Broadway
New York, New York 10018

To the memory
of
Hans Sevcik
Secretary General of the
Austrian Red Cross, 1958–70
who started it all

Chapter 1

May 14, 1978, dawned in Vienna clear, bright and bursting with springtime's equivocal promise. It was a manifestly feminine day. Anything could happen. It was also a Sunday when every sensible person should have been either at church or walking in the Vienna Woods, or having found one of a hundred other good reasons to stay away from the office. By midmorning, Kärntnerstrasse and Stephensplatz were crowded with the customary melange of tourists, the curious, and the faithful drifting vaguely toward the cathedral. In the southeast corner of the Platz, behind the chancel, sightseers meandered, singly and in small groups, dividing their interest between staring up at St. Stephen's gothic spire, like some grotesque medieval road sign pointing the way to heaven, and the innocent contemplation of expensive articles in the windows of the shops. The outsize plate-glass window at number 5B sooner or later caught the eye of most strollers. It was a place of something approaching pilgrimage for art lovers, whether they were college students from San Francisco or aged millionaire collectors from Zurich—all except the abstract enthusiasts, who might have felt out of place here. The only form of advertisement the owner of 5B had ever allowed, and that somewhat grudgingly, was two words etched in large gold letters in the centre of the window: CONWAY WIEN.

The discerning who paused to look through the thick sheet of bullet-proof glass quickly discovered they were looking at objects of great rarity. And great price. In the foreground was, as there always was, a fine china bowl containing a mass of spring flowers. This particular bowl had been made in the Royal Berlin factory about 1780. When it was sold, as it soon would be, another of equal artistry and value would replace it. The price, clearly displayed, was 75,000 Austrian schillings. On either side of the bowl were two paintings, unframed and mounted simply on two unpainted students' easels. The first thing about this arrangement which caught the eye, as it was intended to, was the lighting. The sources, buried in the ceiling above the window, were not just light bulbs, but a highly sophisticated optical system. It was an organ of visual effects upon which its owner, the Hon. Rupert Conway, M.C.—though few these days but the records of his old regiment in Cardiff remembered either the "Hon." or the "M.C."—played with great delicacy. Under his expertise and meticulous taste the pictures came alive.

They were each of the same subject, Madonna and Child, so beloved by the Italian Renaissance painters in which the house of Conway specialized. These two happened to be by the fine, though minor, artist to whom even that fastidious scholar, Bernard Berenson, could put no more authoritative name than "the master of the 'Castello Nativity.'" Minor by Berenson's standards no doubt, but these days the price range for anyone upon whom the great BB had conferred the title "master" starts at fifty thousand pounds in London and higher in New York. The card placed discreetly between the pictures read, "Price by negotiation, to be sold as a pair." There was a challenge to any self-respecting millionaire who thought he knew something about art and value.

The peace and calm which reigned in the Platz outside the window found no kindred serenity inside. Most of the senior members of the establishment were not only working that morning—highly unusual for a Sunday—but were rushing about frantically like raccoons in the mating season. The great man was leaving for New York that afternoon and everyone had been so busy all week that nothing was ready.

Fuming in the kitchen on the second floor, Frau Kröner kept muttering her determination to go to Mass as soon as lunch was over to demonstrate to St. Agnes her contrition for working on Sunday; something she hadn't done since the blessed Sunday in 1955 when the last Russian soldiers evacuated Vienna. That day she had cooked happily for forty-seven people. Today she had already served seven breakfasts, countless cups of coffee and tea, and her entire realm was in a state of turmoil as she prepared lunches for twelve, most of them to be delivered on trays to various parts of the building.

At the switchboard, the indefatigable Mini, Vienna's highest paid and most overworked telephone

3

operator, went about her hectic operations with customary military precision befitting the daughter of a sergeant major of Hussars who in his youth had stood guard outside the bureau of Emperor Franz Josef. Already this morning she had roused a distinguished and irate art dealer from his bed in Greenwich, Connecticut, local time 5 A.M., harried a wealthy English banker off the Sunningdale golf course; and tracked down a Japanese art dealer from Paris who was spending an illicit week-end with an unknown lady in a hotel suite in Geneva. Only her employer's demand to speak to an Austrian official who was spending his week-end chasing chamoix over the mountains in Jugoslavia had defeated her; her Serbo-Croat wasn't quite up to it.

Martita Haupmann, Rupert Conway's secretary, to whom he had dictated seventeen letters in three different languages at machine-gun speed, had sought refuge in her own sanctum and was struggling to decipher her shorthand. She knew from experience there was no point going back to Rupert to check a word. It was his genial habit to instruct her to write in whatever she thought appropriate, having himself long forgotten even to whom he had been writing. Since she had come to him as an untrained, unemployed ingenue shortly after the business opened in 1947, she had only once recorded him as speaking bad grammar—and that was in Spanish, which was neither her own nor Rupert's strong suit. She lived alone and for her work. Who Herr Hauptmann was, or had been, she never volunteered, and Rupert had the delicacy never to enquire. She always addressed him deferentially as "Herr Doktor," the pseudo-title polite Austrians confer on anyone

4

who ever got to a university. In their early days of working together, he had tried addressing her by her first name but such a relationship clearly made her feel uncomfortable. Everybody liked her, and everybody called her "Frau Hauptmann."

Heinz Bergmann was tucked away all by himself in the archives room in the cellar—important art dealers don't keep records; they keep archives—ploughing through old files looking for a letter Rupert was sure he had received from a Professor Toesca, or was it Boesca, of Florence in about 1946—maybe it was 1947. Rupert was sure it contained information about an obscure Renaissance artist called Andrea di Guisto—also sometimes referred to as Guisto di Andrea—and a bundle of photographs he simply must have before leaving for New York. Heinz himself was no scholar. He was a decent, loyal, God-fearing son of a Tyrolean farmer who had been bred never to give up. Though lacking in either inspiration or any kind of intellectual curiosity, Heinz had a knack of finding things which eluded more learned minds by simply applying his limitless patience and inherent mountain cunning. It was a gift which had often been invaluable to Rupert over their many years of association.

Heinz's relationship with Rupert was a uniquely personal one. They had first met lying side by side on stretchers in a British Army advanced casualty station on the icy slopes of Monte Cassino in February 1944. Rupert had just had his right leg blown to pieces from stepping on a landmine while overrunning a line of Austrian trenches which contained, amongst many others, the shell-torn body of Sergeant Heinz Bergmann. When Rupert came to Vienna in May 1945 in charge of the British

5

"MFA" unit—Monuments, Fine Arts and Archives—investigating Nazi art looting, he had chanced to find the ex-sergeant homeless, unemployed and half-starving, and promptly gave him a job as his driver. Ever since that day Heinz had been driving him, running for him, cleaning for him, packing and unpacking for him, and digging for him in any way that appeared to be currently useful.

Heinz and old Max Kallendorf, "the Professor," were the only ones who had ever known the beautiful, pale, young English girl whose silver-framed photograph always sat on the small table next to Rupert's favourite chair in the big drawing room upstairs. They had both been there when he had married her. And they sustained him in his agony of grief when she died in childbirth less than two years later from a dose of polluted penicillin.

Max was spared the tribulations of this unusual day solely because he was in hospital nursing a broken shoulder blade as a result of the latest of his innumerable falls. This time it had been out of a tree which, he cheerfully admitted, was a damn silly place for a nearly blind old man of eighty-two ever to have got himself. But then, it must be acknowledged that Max's week-end world proliferated with grandchildren. His wife, Pauli, a mere girl of seventy-five herself, had never been able to decide whether it was more difficult to protect Max from their grandchildren, or the grandchildren from Max.

Rupert Conway rose early in his handsome bachelor apartment on the floors above the gallery. The apartment was spacious with old-fashioned high ceilings, but its elegance was masculine, reflecting the character of a successful man of taste who had lived alone most of his life. He spent a half-hour carefully packing two large suitcases, one for each stage of his journey, and then listened to the eight o'clock news over breakfast. Nothing seemed to concern him directly. The world appeared to be in its usual turmoil. What else do you expect on the news? The Russians and the Americans were interminably wrangling about something called "Salt." Red terrorists in Italy had shot up a few more innocent people for no reason that made any sense to anyone. The British people were acclimatizing themselves to the idea of a female Prime Minister, and the trade union barons were sulking in their tents. The only piece of news a little closer to home was of a murder somewhere in the Tyrol. Murders are blessedly rare among the civilized Austrians; especially cold-blooded gun murders. Sad for the chap, whoever he was, Rupert thought, but no concern of mine. The weather forecast was good. He folded his linen napkin in a silver ring, bearing the date of his christening and two sets of initials, R.A.D.C., his own; and those of his godfather, R.A.E., which stood for Robert Anthony Eden. Their families had been neighbours in Durban and Rupert's father, the first Lord Gower, a career diplomat, had served under the great Foreign Secretary for many years. Rupert walked leisurely down two flights of stairs and into his office.

Without looking up from the sheaf of papers he was scanning while he opened the door he muttered, "Charlie, get off that chair!" There was a shuffle and a thump as the Welsh terrier removed himself from the tapestry-covered Gainsborough chair which was his favourite forbidden roost, and without the slightest sign of guilt or remorse ambled

7

over under the desk. It was their ordinary routine exchange of civilities.

Seated comfortably behind his Chippendale desk in the office over the front of the gallery, with the cathedral and the broad space of Stephensplatz precisely framed in the window opposite his chair, Rupert Conway was happy as a clam at high tide. Charles Augustus von Conway unt Llangollen, his inseparable companion, slept happily at his feet, from time to time only disturbed by a gentle prod of his master's foot and a peremptory, "Charlie! Stop that disgusting snoring." Just under six feet, no more than comfortably overweight, his robust health scarred only by a slight limp in the right leg, Rupert enjoyed being a successful art dealer with the same enthusiasm as he had enjoyed being a soldier in the Royal Welsh Fusiliers. His room was grey-blue with pipe smoke, the stereo discreetly hidden in the corner was softly churning out his friend Herbert von Karajan's new recording of Mozart's 39th Symphony, and he was ploughing through a pile of papers, most of which interested him enormously. Occasionally he paused, put down his pipe and confided something into the tape recorder at his elbow.

The internal phone on his desk buzzed, without looking up he flipped the winking switch, said, "Hmm," and a husky contralto voice said, "I've found the catalogue for Kate de Rothschild's July exhibition."

"Is the Veronese drawing in it?"

"Number one on her list."

"Put it in my brief case, will you? And remind me to phone Kate in London tomorrow morning. Are my notes ready yet?"

"The girls are just doing the final sorting. Up in ten minutes."

He returned his undivided attention to the papers for a few more minutes and then reached for the microphone.

"Frau Hauptmann, some time while I'm away will you phone Graussinger in Salzburg? Tell him he'll have to bring this porcelain set for me to study. The photographs he sent are very good. I've little doubt it is the Fitzhugh border, and I expect he is right that some of it at least is Chinese export, quite possibly genuine Ching-te Chen, sixteen hundred plus or minus ten years I would think. But I can't commit myself without examining the originals."

The next file contained a long letter about icons. "What does she think I am, a bloody encyclopedia?" he mumbled to himself irritably. He skimmed through the first few pages, the laugh lines under his dark blue eyes showed a trace of impatience, and he rumpled his dark mahogany hair, which showed just the slightest signs of grey at the neck-line. One of his favourite American goddaughters, young Jan Duval from Nantucket, once described him to her room-mate as "a kind of shaggy Christopher Plummer." He reached for the tape again.

"Ask Mrs. Fleming to tell Countess Hoffenstaldt in her sweetest off-putting voice that I can't answer all these tedious questions about her icons. Better check, by the way—I can't remember if we ever sold her any. Tell her to try the Banaki Museum in Athens. If they can't help, somebody at the Byzantine may know what she wants."

Then he came to something which had no difficulty at all grasping and holding his attention. It was a single sheet of stiff white paper, size of a post-

9

card. On it was written in large red block capitals, "Be certain to phone Malcolm Forbes while you're in N.Y. My enquiries make me pretty sure some of the items that Polish refugee talked about really are Fabergé. If so M.F. may be interested. Love, S."

At that moment Sandra Fleming came into the room. To say that Rupert and Sandra were kissing cousins was neither more nor less than the simple truth. He was twenty years older than she was, but she had seized on him as her favourite relation at their first meeting when she was eight years old. Born in Hungary in 1941, fate had decreed a cruel childhood for Alexandra Andrassy. Her mother and Rupert's had been sisters, Viennese. Her father had been Hungarian; Rupert's, Welsh. Their common grandfather, Rudolf Eisenbath, pre-war Vienna's most influential Jewish lawyer had been an early victim of the Nazis. From the day Hitler had forced the Hungarian Regent, Admiral Horthy, to throw his country's lot in with Nazi Germany, the Andrassy family had been hounded and hunted from one end of the Balkans to the other. By the time the British liberated Athens, her father and her four elder brothers and sisters were all dead. It was a common enough story in those days. She and her mother had spent twenty-nine years in the United States, relatively poor, but happy. Most recently she had worked as an assistant archivist at the Metropolitan Museum. The death of her mother and the collapse of a short, disastrous marriage, had both occurred in 1975 at a time when the growth of Rupert's business was beginning to make the employment of a highly qualified archivist a necessity. She had fled to Vienna and "lived with him" ever since; which is to say that she had her own flat above his

10

premises in the back courtyard of the Archbishop's palace, most of which was now rented as offices, or apartments. She had become indispensable to his work and his life.

The entrance of any intruder on Charlie's sleeping time was always resented, but when he looked up and saw who it was he wagged his excuse for a tail, nuzzled her ankle and went back to sleep. Sandra was five-foot-eight, with a figure Rupert liked to describe as "statuesque"; "might have modelled for Donatello's Juno," he once remarked, though whether he saw her naked as the great sculptor had rendered Juno was a secret known only to themselves. Sandra was a rare mixture of aristocratic European breeding and egalitarian American education, and both were twisted just a shade off normal by the tragedy and horror of her childhood years. She was a beautiful woman. Her fastidious taste in clothes matched Rupert's in art. This morning she was wearing an exquisitely fitted St. Laurent dress, a plain chocolate-brown jersey fabric, chic enough to look thoroughly glamorous and practical enough to be businesslike, something she sometimes found difficult. It served as a perfect background for the rather severe, heavy antique gold jewelry she nearly always wore: broach, bracelet and pendant on a long chain. The set had belonged to Rupert's mother, had spent its existence in a bank vault since the day his beloved Alexie died, and he had given it to Sandra on her first Christmas in Vienna.

They smiled affectionately at each other as she sat down in the Gainsborough chair cross from him. She laid a transparent folder of papers on the desk, handed him a leather ticket wallet and picked up the schedule on which she had been working.

11

"Here you are, Mr. Jet Set. Concorde both ways and a suite at Mayfair House. This is going to cost somebody a packet."

Rupert grinned cheerfully.

"You bet your sweet life it is. If Bobby Walker must have me in New York this week to authenticate ten million dollars worth of paintings, he'll darn well pay for it. Bless him!"

He happily lit another pipe, put down the ticket wallet without opening it, and said,

"All these reservations checked?"

She gave him a look of mock indignation.

"You don't think I sat up until after midnight phoning New York, London and Paris for my health do you? Everything is in order."

"Just get the plan clear in my head, will you. I haven't had time to think about it yet."

"Right. You're booked on British Airways to London. God and the unions willing you should be in your club for dinner. I've spoken to the hall porter, a room is reserved for you. Tomorrow morning check-in for Concorde to New York is ten-fifteen. . . ."

"That's going to be tight. I'll have to try to phone Kate de Rothschild tonight. No one knows those Renaissance drawings as she does. Got her home phone number?"

"It's in the file, attached to the papers on the Veronese drawings. What's more I've checked to be sure she'll be there."

That was the sort of service which made Rupert beam with pleasure. He loved being waited on and made no bones about it.

Sandra continued the litany. "Take-off eleven-fifteen, arrive Kennedy at ten local time. Marvelous, isn't it, time goes backwards. Bobby will have a car waiting for you. The driver is a young, sandy-hair fellow who answers to the sname of Syd."

"Great."

"After that you're in Bobby's hands. His secretary has confirmed your hotel. Such information as we have on the Schellenberg collection, not much I'm afraid, is in this file, here." She handed him a file from the folder and lit a cigarette while Rupert browsed through it.

"Old man Schellenberg was never in the first class," he said, "but there's some important stuff here; two Lippis, a Pesellino, Jacopo del Sellaio, Francesco di Antonio. All top of the market these days since practically none of the greats are ever likely to be sold again. The mighty Duveen would have turned up his nose at it, but it's just our line, thank goodness. Funny this lot is so little known. Do I recall Bobby saying the collection has never been shown?"

"That's right. The story, as I understand it, is that Schellenberg made his fortune in the thirties and put the collection together from about nineteen thirty-six to fifty. Since he was blatantly pro-Hitler, he wasn't too popular, even before Pearl Harbor. He was a pariah ever after."

Rupert was studying the file again.

"All these lawsuits. Any information on them? I ought to know something about them."

"Grant Digby in our Chicago office collected all the cuttings from the *New York Times* for you. They go back over five years. Incidentally, when I talked to Grant on Friday he said he had been checking up on the present owner. He says I should warn you. Miss Mary Schellenberg, aged seventy-two, is a very formidable lady. She controls the whole of her late brother's fortune, except what little his secretary got. She's a tough proposition, according to reliable witnesses."

"Not another Nazi, I hope?"

"No. Like most people she apparently loathed her brother's political views. They weren't on speaking terms for years. Just a naturally tough old babe, as Grant so delicately put it."

"I'll read this on the plane."

Sandra glanced at her watch. "It's ten to one. If we don't go up to the dining room for lunch, Frau Kröner is going to quit." The sound of the word "lunch" was enough to rouse Charlie from his slumbers. He shook himself and started to move towards the door. "You've been really driving yourself for weeks, you know. It's a pity this New York trip couldn't be put off till after you've had a break."

"There is too much at stake. Both for Bobby and for me."

"Come and have a relaxed meal while you can."

"Okay. One last thing, most important. How about my return? You can get me to Innsbruck by Friday night? Tony has Cameron and Louise Chambois coming for the week-end, I don't want to miss them."

"No trouble at all, unless you misbehave in Paris. Concorde gets you to Charles de Gaulle at ten forty-five Thursday night. You can be safely in bed at the Ritz before midnight. That is, if you want to, of course. Noon flight to Munich on Friday, change plane and arrive in Innsbruck at four-thirty. Tony will drive over from Schönberg to meet you and you can be safely enthroned in the ancestral schloss for dinner. Anything else?"

14

Rupert knocked out his pipe ashes and rose from his desk. He said very gently, "Just one thing. This is all going to be great fun. I wish you were coming with me."

Sandra betrayed just the hint of a rueful smile as she put the various papers back in the folder and handed them across the desk to him. "Yes," she said, as she stood up, "but, I wasn't invited, and I don't think Bobby would happily double this travel bill. Anyway, you'll be working day and night, and . . . well . . . I don't want to be in New York on my own anymore. Too many memories. With Max in hospital, you away, and only three weeks left to mount the Rome exhibition at the Belvedere . . ."

"I'd completely forgotten about that."

"Somebody better stay home and mind the store."

Charlie was already sniffing impatiently at the door as Rupert opened it. "I understand. But, you know, Tony invited you," he persisted tenderly. "Change your mind and fly up to Schönberg for a few days. You always love the Tyrol, and you can ski right into June now."

"I'll try," she said wistfully. "Maybe your second week-end there. But please, don't make me promise."

They climbed the stairs to lunch just in time to save Frau Kröner from having what the household generally referred to as a "kronery." Cheese soufflé was one of the old lady's great dishes; Rupert had always made it a habit to pay it the esteem it deserved. Charlie kept his nose pressed firmly against his boss's leg, and since Rupert always suffered a guilty conscience when he had to leave his devoted terrier behind, Charlie got more than his fair share of Frau Kröner's *chef d'oeuvre*—fortunately, Frau Kröner never knew.

Sandra's parting greeting with an innocent smile, was, "There is another reason I'm sorry I'm not going."

Rupert raised his heavy eyebrows enquiringly.

"I know you will find time to get to L'Aiglon to eat soft-shelled crabs. Give my love to Guido."

As they drove east across the Stubenring, Heinz handed Rupert a large envelope from Professor Toesca, of Florence.

Chapter 2

At half-past nine the previous evening the traffic winding south over the Europa Bridge towards the Brenner Pass had been light; the usual assortment of vehicles—Mercedes, Volkswagens, Fiats, Citröens and Peugeots—mostly Austrian, Italian and German. A few Chevrolets bearing United States Armed Forces license plates, and the occasional Rolls-Royce with Swiss ones. And trucks. Most of the time most of the movement along the Brenner Motorway these days is trucks. In any normal day police and customs officers at the Austrian/Italian border see trucks from up to sixty countries. The Department of Transportation in Vienna will tell you that one third of Europe's total long-distance freight movements by road goes through the spectacular Alpine gorges between Innsbruck and Bolzano.

A forty-ton twelve-wheeled Berlei carrying license plates with a Leipzig identification from East Germany was just pulling out of the little town of

Gries am Brenner. Gries was a typical picturesque Austrian Alpine village before that monumental feat of modern engineering, the bridge, made this route the Main Street of Middle Europe. Today Gries is one vast concrete pile of roadside pull-ins, gas stations, cafés, souvenir stores and public lavatories. It is the last town before Brenner, where the ascent to the Pass becomes steeper. The lush pine forests, for centuries so dear to the hearts of Austria's Habsburg rulers, begin to thin out and give up the unequal struggle with the snow-clad giants of unforgiving rock. It is also the last place where you can conveniently get off the highway onto the old, twisting Alpine roads that lead to the most remote and unlikely villages, like Obernberg and Vals.

The massive truck was typical of the hundreds which move through the Alps every day plying their trade between East Germany and Italy, most of them carrying meat and dairy products from the state farms in the plains east of Leipzig to the warehouses of Bologna and Milan. As the lights of the town faded behind them, the man sitting next to the driver stubbed out a cigarette and said, "Pull into that lay-by just around the next bend, will you, Heinrich? I have to do something nobody can do for me."

Heinrich smiled and grunted. Just like old Horst, he thought. Always does everything the hard way; we've just passed a dozen service centres. He braked the huge truck/trailer combination gently as they took the broad curve, and had to shift down into first as the road sloped upwards into the tree-lined lay-by where they came to a stop. He reached forward and pulled on the hand brake. Horst lifted his right hand, braced it across his chest, and shot Heinrich just below his right armpit. The nine-millimetre bullet from the Makarov tore straight through his right lung, ripping his heart in shreds, through the door panel and finally lodged itself in a tree on the other side of the highway. He never knew what hit him.

Horst reached over and switched off the ignition. And the lights. He replaced the Makarov in his shoulder holster. It was the new M7 version with which all State Security Officers had recently been equipped. Basically it was still the Russian model which they had copied from the West German Walther, but the new factory just south of Berlin was making parabellum ammunition with a higher powered charge. It was designed to kill at fifty metres. At six inches, its force had lifted Heinrich's great bulk right out of his seat and left his body slumped heavily against the door. Horst had had plenty of practise on the pistol range, but this was the first time he had used it on a job. Its power, combined with remarkable quietness and lack of kick delighted him. A real professional's weapon. Pity about Heinrich. He had quite liked working with him these two years; a dull companion, but reliable, and that counted most in his work. Still, couldn't keep his nose out of other people's business—and got too greedy. They always did, these peasant types.

He buttoned his leather jacket tight so that the gun was virtually invisible against his muscular chest. He looked at his watch. It showed nine forty-two. Fine. It was only a six kilometre walk to Stefan Tolz's cottage just outside Vals, a fine clear evening, and the parcel wasn't heavy. The parcel. The last consignment. That would take a few minutes to extract from its hiding place in amongst the meat cases. It amused him to think that Heinrich had not even known it was there. He regretted he had been a little too open with Heinrich when he first started carrying parcels down into Italy. It was a mistake he rarely made. That was what started the trouble, really, and once Heinrich started blackmailing him, the end was inevitable.

From where they were parked the moon was still blotted out by the massive peak of the Kraxentrager rising nearly three thousand metres from the valley east of the road. In the blackness he could just see the first, faint trace of glistening white slashing the velvet sky where the moonlight was beginning to touch the jagged snow-laden peaks. It would be five to ten minutes yet before it threw any effective light on this side of the mountain. Comfortable time to dig out the parcel, hide the tracks, retie the tarpaulin, and slip unseen through the forest path running down the hillside to the Vals road below. From then on it would be just a pleasant moonlit walk in the country.. How peaceful and unsuspecting these Austrian countryfolk were. Horst was never a naturally happy man, but for the moment he was content—or as near to contentment as he'd ever be.

Fate being the capricious bitch she is, that was the exact moment when things started to go wrong for Horst Rheinberg, until a few moments ago a Hauptmann ("captain" in English) in the Staats Sicherheits Dienstelle—State Security Police—Leipzig Division of the German Democratic Republic, "East Germany."

Vehicles had been passing at a steady rate of two or three every minute, but that didn't worry him. When he got out of the cab he would be completely hidden from the road. The tarpaulin rope was tied at the front off-side corner; he had seen to that little detail. Just as he reached for the door handle and opened it he had two nasty shocks. There was the unmistakable roar of a powerful diesel engine drawing up into the lay-by immediately behind the Berlei, and its dazzling headlights were pointing at the exact spot where he urgently wished to be. He was well trained to deal with a situation like this, but what was required at the moment was not another murder. He had to retrieve the parcel, and he had to get out of Austria with it as fast as possible. Above all, as secretly as possible. He had learned that from reading the files. Without total secrecy you hadn't a hope. Once your new cover was broken, they would hunt you down to the ends of the earth.

The rumbling died as the driver switched off his engine. Horst held his breath a few seconds hoping he would switch off the lights as well. He didn't. Damn him! Horst bent double and ducked into the black hole between the back of the cab and the body of the trailer. Above the sound of the pine trees whispering their secrets to the night he heard a metal door open and close again. Someone got out. Voices were speaking German, but the glare of the headlights made it impossible for him to see the license plate. Were they Austrian? German? East or West? Did it matter? Wait and see was all he could do. There appeared to be at least two men. Could be three. What were they going to do next? He swore vehemently to himself as he heard a voice from inside the cab call to the man now on the roadside, "Ask the fella up ahead."

Horst knelt on one knee and watched the legs of a man walking along the length of the trailer clearly

21

lit up in the glare of his mate's headlights. The legs stopped beside the driver's door and his blood congealed as he heard a cheerful voice call out, "Hi, up there! Have you got a nine-millimetre spanner in your kit?"

There was silence again for a moment, broken only by the whirr of a passing car. Then he heard the man, standing only a couple of metres away from him, mutter, "That's funny." The man in the truck behind called out, "Anything wrong, Karl?"

At that moment Karl must have reached up and opened the cab door. There was a piercing scream, and then a succession of heavy thumps as Heinrich's body rolled out of the cab and landed a dead weight right on Karl's head and chest. The two men, one dead and one alive, fell in a tangled heap of arms and legs onto the asphalt while the two holes in Heinrich's massive chest spurted blood all over both of them.

A door slammed and another man came running. "Karl, what the hell . . . !"

Horst had no choice left but to run for cover in the woods. There was no light this side of the truck and the tree line was only a few metres away.

He made it in one quick sprint, dropping gently and noiselessly into the undergrowth. His keen trained eyes and ears quickly reassured him: The two men, surprised and shocked by the horror of disentangling from Heinrich's bleeding corpse, had been far too preoccupied to have noticed him.

His Division Commander back in Leipzig would have been proud of him, but his Division Commander and Leipzig were the farthest things in the world from Horst's thoughts as he lay in the temporary security of those bushes, every sense strained to understand exactly what was going on at the other side of the truck. Leipzig was the past; the future started here. There must be some opportunity to get back and retrieve that parcel. Perhaps it was going to be necessary to kill these two interfering fools as well.

His hand reached softly under his leather coat and undid the buttons that concealed the Makarov under his left armpit. There would still be seven rounds in it.

Suddenly the lights of the Berlei came on. One of them must have climbed up into the cab. That wouldn't do him any good, but the additional light was not exactly welcome either. He couldn't see the other man, but from the excited shouts going back and forth it seemed he was out on the edge of the highway trying to flag down a passing motorist.

His ears caught the unmistakable throb of a heavy diesel shifting gears down to negotiate the rising slope of the hill. He cursed under his breath. That one would stop, all right. Of whatever nationality, the European knights of the road are a close and mutually supportive body of men these days.

It stopped. Killing four more men was beyond all reason. And probably all hope. Horst quietly rose to his feet and made his careful way through the wooded slope down to the road below.

Over all of the Alpine massif Sunday, May 14 was the kind of day the authors of travel brochures pray for. The sort of day when their most wildly optimistic superlatives really do come true. As the sun came over the mountains into a nearly cloudless sky the air temperature started to climb. And so did the people. By nine o'clock the more ambitious skiers

23

and climbers were sweating, and by noon many of the younger aficionados would be baring their chests to the sun and the hoped-for admiration of their girl friends.

As the sun climbed higher, the snow-clad mountains, the green pasture land beneath them, the countless small villages and lakes and streams took on a mirage-like quality, a constantly changing surrealist montage. Every few moments another snow-crowned peak, silhouetted against the sky in tones ranging from translucent ultramarine to sombre purple, suddenly burst into flame and within a few minutes passed through the spectrum until it finally emerged a glistening white as though covered with freshly laundered satin sheets.

In Austria, Italy and Switzerland it was just the sort of day when every tourist department photographer would be out ecstatically taking pictures of a beautiful girl in a bikini mounted on the shoulders of some fully clad virile young Adonis on skis. The international battalions of motorists, cyclists, hikers, climbers and skiers started mounting the slopes, while the amateur flyers were taking to the skies in light aircraft, gliders, parachutes and the newest, most exhilarating and dangerous of all sports, hang gliders. From the pilot's seat in a glider at an altitude of two thousand metres Horst Rheinberg probably had as grand a view as anyone alive that morning.

After Tolz had launched him into the air he had headed straight for Lake Olperer where he had picked up, as he knew he would on any reasonable flying day, a series of strong thermals, upward currents of warm air known in the Tyrol as *föhns*, which, with skilled navigation, had lifted him up well over two thousands metres. His only problem at this stage was traffic. Every other Sunday flyer from the three small gliding clubs in the vicinity had the same idea. Having circled to the top of the *föhn* he then turned south and, as he came round in a wide arc gaining speed, he could see at least twenty other fixed-wing craft and hang gliders performing similar manoeuvres below him. Even Horst's jaded soul could not resist some passing sense of joy from the beauty of this aerial ballet.

Had he been so inclined he could have simply sat there and admired the constantly changing spectrum of views. For a moment he was presented with a romantic, oblique angle view of the hermitage of St. Bernhard on the northern slope of Kraxentrager. Only a few years ago five monks, bound by solemn vows to a life of hardship and austerity, lived in the medieval hospice, their only contact with fellow mortals being in the course of rescuing lost or exhausted climbers. Now the picturesque old building houses a shelter for skiers, complete with central heating and a well-stocked coffee bar. To the east below the new hamlet of Wiszenthal he could see the azure sparkle of the new lake formed by a massive wall of concrete soaring four hundred metres up the wooded mountainsides damming up millions of tons of water to generate hydro power destined to wind its way through high-tension cables as far away as Vienna, Zurich and Milan. When the monks left St. Bernhard the valley was nothing but tiny streams tumbling down to join the Inn.

A man not so completely absorbed in his own thoughts might have marvelled at many of these prodigious contrasts which nature, transfigured by the restless invention of man, has been forced to display for man's own edification. The Zillertaller and the Dolomite ranges present a kaleidoscope of fantasy beyond anything the most imaginative nineteenth-century toymaker ever dreamed of; savage white peaks, lethal grey cliffs and gentle, green, smiling meadows all thrown together higgledy-piggledy in a giant's punchbowl. A man only slightly less cynical than Horst might have been strangely impressed by the startling paradox which flashed past his line of vision as a group of some dozen hang gliders—*drachenflieger* as they are so allusively called in the Tyrol—hurled themselves off the edge of a precipice a thousand metres above the valley of the river Tuxertal and flew directly over the heads of a procession of farmers driving their flower bedecked cattle up a winding grassy path to summer pastures. It is an ancient custom of the Tyrolese to plait the animals' heads and horns with spring flowers for this annual pilgrimage—to ward off evil spirits which might be lurking in the high grasslands above the timber line.

These colourful sights were lost on Horst. From one point of view this solitary route over the Alps was about the most dangerous and precarious he could have chosen. For anyone who was not a skilled glider pilot it would have been impossible. That may have been one reason it had always appealed to him. In his mind it was the most secure because the most secretive route, and secrecy would be the only guarantee of preserving his life, during the period of transition to the new existence he had for so long dreamed about, so carefully planned. Horst, like everyone else in East Germany, had been a cynic since early youth. No one, from members of the Polit-bureau on down, any longer believed in anything except survival and the cruel reality of Russian military power. Over half a million of them brandished their guns and armour right under your nose every moment of the day. Like everyone else in the GDR he had often brooded on the prospect of escaping to some kind of freer life. After a while it was the sheer grey hopelessness of life under Communism that weighed one down. Practically no one in the Soviet Satellite countries over the age of sixteen smiles very much. God has been abolished. Marx has turned out to be a fraud. What remains is now popularly called "Goulash Communism"—dull, tasteless and highly indigestible.

Horst simply wanted to get out. Not for any passionate ideological reasons; like most people in most countries he didn't have any definable ideology, just a longing to survive and a stubborn prejudice to want to do it in his own way. He was no deep political thinker, and insofar as he had read the words and thoughts of western politicians and intellectuals they seemed to him to be about as befuddled and remote from the aspirations of ordinary folk as the Marxist kind he was forced to applaud at home. He had joined neither the party nor the SSD from any sense of political conviction, nor even much interest. It was a means of survival, and he could buy simple luxuries, like real coffee, or oranges, only available at the Delikat and Exquisit shops reserved for the party élite. If you have to live with a tiger to survive, better to ride it than be stalked by it; at least the odds against falling foul of the party bosses were slightly less. If you have to kill someone, well, you kill him. There is no heaven; hell is here and now. There was nothing he could do about it.

Cynicism may just possibly lead to a way out, but

it seldom breeds heroes. Horst never had any desire to make newspaper headlines for a week and then spend the rest of his life begging the CIA for protection. His ambition was much simpler than that. All he wanted was a modest farm somewhere in the Argentine where he could grow grapes. Both his father and his grandfather had been vintners. There is always good money in making wine. All it required were the skills he had been brought up with back in the vineyards of Franconia, and a little capital to get started. He knew where to acquire that. Every day when he was in Italy he had studied the newspapers for reports of auction sales in the international art market. Only last month he had read that a Francesco Pesellino had sold in London for thirty-two thousand pounds. He had two canvases by Pesellino hidden in the ceiling of his Bologna apartment: not the one which was his operating headquarters, but another little one-room affair down the street, which was nobody's business but his own. Paris, they had told him. That's where the business is, they said. Every major defector caught smuggling art works out of the country had been heading for Paris. He had never been there, but he had been studying it for years. He hadn't wasted those two tedious years working in the Criminal Records Department in Berlin.

When Moscow had pushed the puppet government of East Berlin into the job of front-line support for the Italian Red Brigade terrorists, he had found the perfect role in which to work out his long dreamed of objective; a safe exit for himself and his "capital." For the last two years he had been going back and forth between Leipzig and Bologna every few weeks in the guise of a truck driver's mate, and every time he had a consignment of fine paintings ready, he had hidden them away in his personal luggage. He had also served his masters well. During his frequent sojourns in Italy he had wormed his way into the very heart of the *brigatista* organization as friend, adviser and trusted supplier of the weapons of death and mutilation. Well hidden amongst the crates of meat he and Heinrich had ferried through the Brenner Pass had been countless others containing hundreds of the deadly Scorpion machine pistols from Czechoslovakia—like the one they used to butcher Aldo Moro—reliable 43/52 sub-machine guns from Poland, Russian Dragunov sniper's rifles and the vicious V40 fragmentation grenades, the smallest and most lethal hand grenade ever invented. Never once had they been stopped or interfered with by anybody. If Moscow had ordered them to supply the terrorists with nuclear weapons, nobody would have lifted a finger to stop them. Everybody in free Europe was too busy.

At the start of the mission Horst had worked closely with Renato Curcio, the muddle-headed dehumanized Trento University sociologist who had instigated the first wave of Red Brigade killings with terrible and increasing ferocity. After Curcio had been captured in 1976 Horst had become the trusted confidant of Corrado Alunni, the mastermind of more than thirty killings, kidnappings and mutilations since he assumed command of that body of fanatics and misfits. Together they had plotted every detail of the capture of Aldo Moro, five times Prime Minister of Italy and "beloved" of Pope Paul VI. At this critical moment he was one of the few people who knew exactly where Alunni was, as well as the details of the next spectacular kidnapping

Alunni had planned. The mock trial and phony judicial murder of Moro had been the most audacious and perfectly planned operation of the entire struggle. As a professional secret service officer assigned by his government to support a major terrorist campaign, he had a professional's pride in his handiwork. It had been totally successful. The fact that the outcome was not as had been expected; that the entire Italian working class had been outraged rather than delighted by its pitiless cruelty; that the Communist parties of every country in Western Europe, including the Italian, had been revolted by the useless slaughter; that the deed had, for the moment at any rate, united their enemies closer than ever before; all this was the result of political miscalculation, and politics was not his business. The fact that their Russian masters had, for once, got cold feet and were now engaged in dragging back control of the whole operation into their own hands had been the unmistakable signal that the time had arrived for Horst to disappear. Even Alunni had no inklings of his private plans.

The lowest point in the ridge running due east from Brenner was now only a couple of kilometres ahead. He was bound to lose a few hundred metres in height as he approached it, but he also knew that any minute now he would hit a "ridge-lift," an area where the wind blowing against the knife edge of rock and snow would be diverted directly upwards, lifting him sufficiently high again to clear the crest. That crest was the Italian border. On the other side of it was an easy drift down to the high pastures above the little village of San Jacopo. He had practised the manoeuvre three times last summer, and this time he had no need to worry about finding another current to take him back again.

With a hundred metres to spare he cleared the crest, the only critical moment of the flight. Once over the frontier he found, as one expected in that area, a gentle southwesterly prevailing breeze that would carry him slowly and uneventfully over these barren southern-facing slopes already nearly denuded of snow, for an easy landing in the secluded meadow behind Mario Lugano's isolated farm less than ten kilometres ahead. He knew Mario would not be there.

Looking round him in this new landscape he was reassured to see that he shared the air space with enthusiasts from the Brunico and Bressanone gliding clubs who were also taking advantage of the perfect flying conditions. Gliding has become a major sport in many parts of the Alps, so no one would notice one plane more or less on a Sunday.

With ample altitude and another twenty minutes of carefree flying ahead of him Horst let his mind wander over the events of last night. It was a pity he had had to abandon that last consignment of valuable canvases in the truck but, with two intercontinental juggernauts parked in the lay-by with all their lights burning, and four excited men milling around there was just no opportunity to retrieve them. When he had heard the siren of a police car racing up the valley he knew there was no way of going back. He had had no trouble finding one of the many stony paths leading down off the autobahn, through the lightly timbered woods below, and in due course out onto the winding mountain road that led to Vals.

31

Stefan Tolz, the disgruntled mechanic and social misfit, with a criminal record stretching back to his boyhood in Bregenz, lived alone in a gloomy cottage just outside the village. He was a surly and grudging man, and in the tightly knit little society of an endogamous Tyrolean community he had no trouble keeping to himself. During the day he worked in a garage down at Gries. On his days off he went gliding, and when he was paid enough he kept a safe house for the East German-Red Brigade network. He hadn't much, but it was everything needed for Horst's operations. Stefan had been expecting him. Stefan asked no questions. Horst's only annoyance was that at the last minute Stefan had raised the price demanded for the glider, but he had anticipated that.

As the first view of San Jacopo appeared ahead of him Horst glanced at the altimeter and noticed that he had descended to a little under five hundred metres. Provided the wind held its strength and direction it was enough to take him over the village, across the small rushing stream and clear the pine woods that hid Mario's lonely farm from the rest of the scattered little community. He could clearly see the unpaved mountain road winding up from Bressanone, the neat meadows spread out each side of it, the vegetable gardens and occasional small vineyards which helped the highland farmers eke out a passable living in this inhospitable terrain. The inevitable onion-spired white stucco church was a little farther east than he would have liked it and he altered course accordingly. As he studied the ground, it crossed his mind for the first time that the altimeter was perhaps not as accurate as it should have been. Of course not. Damn! The barometric pressure on the south side of the ridge would almost certainly be different from that on the north, but he had no idea what the correction that morning might be. To his practised eye the space immediately beneath him did not look like five hundred metres. More like three. Or even two-fifty. He had been losing height too rapidly and realized he would need more to carry him through the inert air he was sure to meet over the pine wood. The only obvious place to find another *föhn* would be over the river itself, and that lay too far west. He trimmed his craft as tightly as he dared and hoped for one more upward thrust from somewhere.

The glider skimmed over the wide-angled roof of the little inn on the northern edge of San Jacopo at a height of no more than a hundred and fifty metres, losing height rapidly as the wind died away. Horst could clearly make out details of the clothing of the small group of people involved in some kind of ceremony in the nearby churchyard. It was too late now to change course and try to skirt the pine wood, the very act of turning would cause him to lose height faster. There were too many people around the ground was too stony to permit a safe landing here. Another few minutes and he was over a dense mass of pine trees. He sensed rather than felt an almost complete lack of lift beneath him and the fall of the altimeter reading confirmed it. There were only a few hundred metres to go but it was going to be a near run thing.

He felt no sense of fear or even danger; nor did he care a hoot about what happened to the glider. It had fulfilled its purpose and he had no further use for it. But it was years since he had crash landed and the thought of it hurt his pride as a pilot. He

33

should have noticed the danger in time to take action. It was too late now. Then he spotted a small clearing straight ahead and risked lifting the glider's nose just a fraction. His guess was right and she responded, quickly rising a precious five or six metres. Then he was travelling through the inert air above the trees again.

He wasn't going to make it. Another few seconds and he had to let the nose come down to avoid a stall. A minute later and he could hear the unmistakable swishing of topmost branches against the bottom of the glider's hull. He judged he was still doing between ten and fifteen knots. As long as the branches were thin enough and supple enough he still had an outside chance. At that moment something firmer and tougher scraped along the bottom and tore a gash in the fabric of the tail-plane. The control stick kicked out of his hands, the star-board wing dropped lurching into the thicker foliage of the treacherous pines. A vagrant gust caught the under side of the sky-seeking port wing, and the entire fuselage somersaulted into the trees. His protective arm movements were not quite quick enough. The momentum of the crash threw him forwards over the front of the cockpit and his head collided with a tree. He felt his body lurch clear of the disintegrating air-frame and then the successive blows as it tumbled and bounced crazily down from branch to branch. The blood from the gash in his forehead ran into his eyes and blinded him. Then he hit the ground and blacked out.

Chapter 3

A good night's sleep in his London club always uplifted Rupert's spirits and massaged his deeply conservative nature. It was the only place he knew where nothing ever changed except for the better—they had modernized the plumbing in bedroom six for the first time since Queen Victoria died—or perhaps since she was born!

In the first half-hour after take-off he had satisfied himself that flying at eleven hundred miles an hour really did feel exactly like flying at six hundred, or one hundred for that matter, and since he didn't feel like drinking champagne at this time of the morning he spent an uninterrupted three hours studying the papers in his attaché case. Although he was Austrian and Welsh by birth, he appeared every inch the English businessman, complete with his dark blue London felt hat and very English mackintosh in case of rain. Nothing was missing except the umbrella. By the time the sandy-haired Syd deposited him outside Walker's Gallery at 720 Madison Avenue he felt fully in command of himself and the situation he was about to confront.

After a momentary pause to admire the eighteenth-century Dutch landscape by Gerhard Hendricks which graced the window, he walked unhurriedly through the opulent salon and took the elevator to the third-floor offices where Bobby Walker presided over one of America's most prestigious art businesses. Their friendship dated from childhood school days in Washington when Rupert's father had been third secretary at the British embassy, and Bobby's had taught history of art at Washington and Lee University. Throughout their lives their careers had been frequently and curiously intertwined and their relationship mellowed to a fine vintage. As his father doggedly climbed the protocol trail from embassy to embassy, from Vienna to Paris to Rome to Stockholm, Rupert's mother had introduced him to the world's great art galleries. No dedicated teacher ever had a more enthusiastic pupil. Bobby had reached Paris as an art student just in time to taste the dying legend of Montmartre. Both men had ended the Second World War ferreting round Alpine castles and salt mines after the treasures buried there by the two biggest art looters in history: Hitler and Goering.

Now both nearing sixty they were at the peak of a profession which admirably suited their style and temperament; they looked exactly what they were, civilized, successful and sensibly contented. Bobby was slightly the leaner, the greyer and the richer, which is probably not a bad measure of the difference between living in Manhattan and in Vienna.

Ten minutes later a security guard locked both of them into a sparsely furnished gallery that took up most of the seventh floor where Walker's finest treasures were housed. There were no windows, the walls being entirely covered by huge panels of velvet in five different colours ranging from pale grey through bottle-green, light blue and dark blue, to black. They were hung on aluminum rails from the roof so they could be readily shifted to produce whatever backdrop the proprietor thought most suitable. The optical lenses set in the drop-ceiling were so subtly hidden that the light appeared almost to emanate from the canvases themselves. In the middle of the room three eighteen-branch Waterford chandeliers cast an elegant glow over a twenty-foot mahogany conference table—which had cost eleven thousand dollars in 1949—which was piled high with papers, catalogues, reference books, photographs and associated optical paraphernalia. The most important items of the late Walter Schellenberg's collection lined the walls. The velvet panels backing them were black.

Two photographers and a girl, all dressed like cowboys, had their equipment sprawled all over one end of the big room. A studious-looking man in his early thirties with thick glasses and a badly worn tweed jacket was examining a canvas with a magnifying glass and dictating his comments to a plump, cherubic-faced secretary. As the boss and his entourage entered the gallery the plump girl disappeared and the young man came over to greet them.

Bobby Walker said, "This is Henry Kovalick who is in charge of cataloguing for us. Henry, meet the famous Rupert Conway."

Rupert extended his hand in his usual firm, friendly manner and said, "Forget the famous stuff, Henry. Glad to meet you."

37

At a signal from Walker's secretary the photographers put down their innumerable bits of gadgetry, switched off their lighting equipment, and the guard checked them out the security door. The plump girl returned with a new note pad and took up a defensive position behind Henry. The rest of the party consisted of Frank Rogerson, Yale, Accademia del Roma and eight years at the Huntington Gallery in Los Angeles, Walker's executive vice-president, art; and Bill Sparkman, University of Southern California, Price Waterhouse and seven years at Citibank of New York, his financial comptroller.

Bobby Walker led everyone to the conference table and opened the proceedings.

"Time's short. Miss Schellenberg flies into town tomorrow night. She's due here nine A.M. Wednesday morning, and God help us! Mr. Conway has to leave Thursday morning for the Tyrol. So, we have just two days to decide on how to cope with the lady, and agree on the final draft of Mr. Conway's notes for the catalogue. Most of it is reasonably straightforward. I think you agree, Henry?"

Henry nodded.

"But there are some doubtfuls, Rupert. Some very doubtfuls, and we can't start printing the catalogue until they're decided."

Henry nodded vigorously.

"I think you know a bit about the checkered history of the collection," Walker was now talking to Rupert. "There it is, but we still haven't got her signature, on a contract, and after seven years of lawsuits the old witch is getting mighty impatient. She won't sell it to me. She insists it will make more money at auction—of course she's right—and I can't auction it until we are absolutely certain of the provenance, and you have written your opinion of every picture in it."

"Something like ten million dollars worth, you said?" Rupert enquired, glancing round the walls.

"Now that we've had a chance to study it, more like fifteen," Bobby replied, flicking an offending cigarette ash off his pin-stripe Brooks Brothers suit.

Rupert wished he had had time to come on the Queen Elizabeth II and take two suites at Mayfair House.

"And you expect me to authenticate all of it in two days?" he said.

Bobby looked across at Henry Kovalick and nodded him his cue.

"The problem is not quite so bad as it sounds, Mr. Conway." Henry had a funny habit of taking off his glasses and talking through them as though he had a microscopic tape recorder hidden on one ear piece. (Later in the day he left them on the table for a few minutes and Rupert was disappointed to discover he hadn't.)

"Most of the documentation is first class," Henry continued. "We've prepared all the ground for you, so I hope you'll find most of it is plain sailing. I've hung everything we are reasonably certain of—where the papers, provenance and my own experience give me confidence—along those three walls. All their documentation is in that big pile. Mr. Walker and Mr. Rogerson have both confirmed my opinions. We bow to your judgement, of course, but I don't think it will present any serious problems. The ones on the end wall—their papers on the small table over there—are the headaches."

39

Rupert nodded approvingly, and ignoring the "No Smoking" signs prominent all round the room started to fill his pipe.

Without a word Walker's decorous secretary opened a drawer and placed a large cut-glass ashtray in front of him. The smile of relief on Sparkman's face as he took out his own pipe was an instant declaration of alliance.

Bobby asked, "Do you want to look at them straight away, Rupert?"

"If you don't mind, there are rather a lot of questions I'd like to ask first. My judgement is usually a bit more acute if I feel I understand the background."

"Fire away. We've nothing more important to do for the next three days than make Miss Schellenberg happy."

"And that's not easy, I'm told. Perhaps for a start someone might brief me on the mysterious Mr. Schellenberg; his motivation, his buying policy if there ever was one; how he put it together and why."

Bill Sparkman obviously handled all such matters in the Walker establishment.

"Yeah. Well, I better start at the beginning then. As I have the story, old father Schellenberg left Germany and settled in Wisconsin about the turn of the century. Started as a logger and gradually built up a nice little timber business of his own. Like a lot of immigrants in those days he was more or less illiterate and never learned to speak much English. He died somewhere in the twenties and left his business to his son and daughter jointly. That's when the family feuding really started. The son, Walter, was a chip off the old block. He went to work in the mill at fourteen and knew nothing about anything except wood. And money, of course. He knew a lot about that. Sister Mary went off to school in Milwaukee and became a lady. Neither of them married.

"In nineteen thirty-three Walter developed a new process for making plywood and the money started rolling in. The family lawyers told me he did everything he could to get hold of his sister's shares. Tried to buy her out, but she wouldn't sell. Tried to squeeze her out, but she sued him. So, as the old buzzard became a millionaire, so did she. They really hated each other, by all accounts.

"As I told your man in Chicago, Schellenberg was a blatant admirer of Hitler, had his picture hung in his office, used to go over to the party rallies at Nürnburg. When the war came along the government put an administrator in to run the business, but the profits still belonged to the shareholders, so they both got richer and richer. Walter got control back again in nineteen forty-six, and she still hung on. He never did get her out.

"Then in nineteen sixty-nine he developed cancer. When he knew he was dying he married his secretary, but he died only a few weeks later without ever making a will. The secretary claimed his share, his abortion of a mansion, and his art collection. Mary sued, naturally, and after five years of legal wrangling, Mary won."

"There is no challenge to her ownership now?" Rupert interrupted.

"None whatever. She promptly sold the business—got over twenty million for it so they say—tore the house down and then announced she was giving the pictures to the state art gallery. While the lawyers were dealing with that little matter there

41

was a change of governor, and she didn't like the new one so she changed her mind. The new governor said she couldn't, so everybody sued everybody else again—real paradise for the lawyers, this was. Mary won, as usual. Now, she hates the pictures, all she wants to do is sell them to the highest bidder and pocket the cash. Bobby made her the most attractive offer, so there they are, and one way or another we've got to sell them and take our profit before she thinks up some reason to sue us."

"Has she any grounds?"

"No way. At the moment. But, as Bobby said, she hasn't signed anything yet, and if we don't get the sale moving quickly she's perfectly capable of bringing the bailiffs in here and hauling them all away again."

Bobby interjected. "That would be very embarrassing."

"And this is May fifteen," Rupert said. "So we have six weeks or leave it till after Labor Day."

"God forbid," said Bobby with deep feeling.

Rupert nodded sympathetic understanding.

"Now tell me why the collection," he said.

Sparkman scratched his rapidly balding dome. Everybody else just sat and looked at him. Then he put down his pipe and said, "I've spent weeks thinking about that, and I'm not sure I can give you an answer. This is just my own figuring. Even his lawyers don't know, but that's not really surprising because he was always changing them. It's an odd fact, but true so far as I can find, that about the only human being Schellenberg ever admired, other than Hitler, was Henry Clay Frick. Not very flattering for Mr. Frick I guess, but it's not his fault. Probably Frick's epic battles against the unions endeared him to Schellenberg, since he had more strikes than anyone else in the state. He wasn't in Frick's class, and there's no evidence he ever met him, but we found two books of press cuttings in his files; one on Frick's art collecting, and another on his business. My guess is that he decided to collect pictures as Frick had done, but being the miserable creature he was, he did it in such a way that nobody but himself was ever going to get any pleasure out of it. That would account for the fact that he never allowed the collection to be shown; maybe why he never made a will."

They spent the rest of the morning going through some of the gems in the collection, and as Henry had said, Rupert found nothing to trouble him. He was satisfied they were exactly what they claimed to be; the Lippis, Michelinos, Sellaios, Jacopo Franci; amongst the best of the Italian Renaissance artists whom Mellon, Frick and Morgan and their generation had not already bought up and subsequently presented to public art galleries in memory of themselves. Rupert's opinion of Henry Kovalick continued on a rising curve. He was not, certainly, a physically impressive man but he undoubtedly knew his business. Together they inspected such obscure details as human hair and ears and hands—it is amazing how many famous artists never mastered the techniques of painting ears and hands, while no two great masters ever painted hair in quite the same way. They applied their magnifying glasses to the folds in drapery and clothing, those inexplicable swaths of unsupported cloth draped around the intimate parts of otherwise naked humans, defying gravity and held up by some esoteric mechanism still undiscovered. The way in which an artist painted the texture of trees in the background, or frequently did not bother to paint them, is another amongst the long list of abstruse items the public seldom notice but which are the usually nearly fool-proof signatures by which all artists in every age have unconsciously declared their identity to scholars, thus exposing countless fakes and forgeries. All the great artists throughout history—Michelangelo, Rembrandt, Botticelli, Titian, Raphael—had their own peculiar tricks and techniques to deal with such minutiae that the student or the copier finds it almost impossible to duplicate.

At twelve thirty-two smiling Filipino waiters were ushered through the security screen bearing silver trays of fresh chicken and smoked salmon sandwiches generously garnished with watercress, olives and celery. Walker's secretary pressed a button somewhere under the table and a black-velvet curtain slid noiselessly out of sight revealing a fully stocked bar from which the head Filipino produced two well-chilled bottles of a particularly fine 1972 Montrachet. The secretary, whose name was Jenny, handed round cut-crystal wine glasses and filled them with a certain panache that made Rupert wonder whether she liked soft-shelled crabs.

"In your honour," Bobby said to Rupert. "For ordinary visitors we usually serve Löwenbrau."

After lunch they got down to the major problems. Some of them were easier than expected. A work which was attributed to Luca di Tomme in Rupert's opinion undoubtedly was. To Bobby Walker's surprise he said he thought it a rather good one.

"Well, that's a relief," Bobby said. "I had it in the back of my mind you didn't think much of Luca."

44

"I didn't."

"Didn't you once write a review saying he was 'chocolate box,' or something like that?"

"Yes, I did," Rupert replied blandly. "But I changed my mind."

"You changed your mind?" Bobby said with genuine surprise.

"Yes, I did. Years ago, you know, I learned it was a very good habit to change my mind whenever I came to the conclusion I was wrong."

There was nothing more to be said about Luca di Tomme.

One claiming to have been painted by Andrea Vanni he felt would be better labeled "Sienese school, circa 1400."

Exhibit C raised a new question altogether. It was a figure of Christ by the river Jordan painted on wood. The bill of sale and the provenance had been provided by a dealer in Philadelphia in 1938 and claimed it to be a missing panel from a thirteenth-century altarpiece by Niccola di Segna.

After nearly fifteen minutes with the magnifying glass, Rupert finally said, "Not bad. Not at all bad. Niccola's style all right, nice brushwork, good detail. But the wood is all wrong, isn't it?"

Henry Kovalick smiled and looked across at Walker for support. "I knew you would spot that, but Bobby told me I mustn't say anything which might influence your judgement."

Rupert chuckled contentedly. "He was quite right. You've checked it?"

"Artistically, as far as we could," Henry addressed his glasses in his most confidential manner. "Two known panels from the same altar are right here in New York, in a private collection. If the

45

painting isn't Niccola's, it's a very good copy. If it weren't for the wood I'd say 'school of.' "

"The wood doesn't necessarily make it a fake. It's a problem of date and place, isn't it. Any idea what it is?"

"No. We've tried all the obvious ones, olive, various Italian fruit woods. We found a walnut from Cyprus that was close. What's your guess?"

Rupert took the picture to the table and turned it over. With a small pen knife he made a shallow scratch on the back. He examined it closely under the magnifying glass. Then he scraped a bit more, rubbed the shreds of wood together between his fingers, and smelled them. Then he put a few grains on his tongue and tasted them.

"Bought in Philadelphia, you said?"

"Here is the bill of sale."

"What does the dealer say?"

"He died in nineteen thirty-nine. Company long been out of business."

"Well, you better get a wood expert in here pretty quick. But, since it came from Philadelphia, I think I'm going to stick my neck out on this one, just a little. I met something like this in Los Angeles three, maybe four years ago. I'm going to guess, guess mind you, that this is hickory . . . and if it is, you know what that means."

No one in Europe could possibly have painted on hickory until many years after the first voyage of Christopher Columbus, but somebody had claimed this was a hundred years earlier.

"First time I've come across that one," Henry said.

Bobby asked, "What do you think it is then, Rupert?"

ent in comfort. "As Henry so
a whole new ball game indeed.
us to believe that the great Joe him-
ed in the affairs of poor little An-

Bobby said. "I think it would be
o say, some one wanted Schellen-
."

e no doubt at all about the purpose
t testified that the incomparable
n was of the opinion that the Ma-
d with two angels was indeed the
f one Andrea di Guisto, "a minor
nter," and that they had recently
man in Paris.

y, isn't it," Rupert said. "Here we
genuine picture, of no importance
sity value, and someone goes to all
manufacturing a blatantly phony
t wouldn't fool anyone with an
owledge in these matters."

'As far as I know there is no evi-
erg ever acquired any real knowl-
ight pictures if they seemed impres-

no name in the trade more impres-
en," Rupert said.

very hesitantly, "You're still certain
nuine?"

ng up from his study of the unbe-
his hand Rupert said, "Oh yes. No

time they all looked at him in
silence. Rupert continued, "Some

"Well, I'm talking straight from memory, and I've only seen a hickory panel like this once. You know, some of the old planter families in the South used to own fine Italian paintings. In the Civil War a lot disappeared—destroyed, looted, the usual story. Then there was a man called Reynolds, I think it was. You can look him up. He studied in Italy and was working in Virginia at the end of the eighteen sixties. Actually, he was a very fine painter, but he specialized in copying Italian styles and selling them to gullible Northerners. It was much more profitable. Can't blame him really, can you? So, if your wood expert says that's hickory, I would suggest we catalogue it as an early American reproduction—that's a more respectable word than fake."

Jenny left in a hurry to dig up a wood expert.

The next picture was not so much a problem as a joke. It was an enormous nude; the lady's vital statistics were of the order of forty-six, thirty-six, fifty. Not centimeters. Inches.

"What's it supposed to be?" Rupert asked.

Henry handed him a folder in which he read, "School of Rubens, probably by the master, finished by one of his pupils, circa 1600."

"Balls!" Rupert grunted. "The quintessence of balls."

Bobby smiled, "Yes, quite. But, what is it?"

"Well, there is just everything wrong, isn't there? In 1600 Rubens didn't have a school—he was in Mantua painting for the Duke. Then he went to Rome to paint for the Pope. He didn't do many nudes for either of those gentlemen, and he certainly never painted anything like this in his life. Look at it! The body is late nineteenth-century bar-room art. What Renoir called the advanced state of broad-hipped pregnancy. Sort of thing Toulouse-Lautrec might have done late one night while drunk as a hoot owl. But he would have the good taste to tear it up next morning. And the face! Twentieth-century degenerate. Even Hermann Goering wouldn't have bought this. Where on earth did Schellenberg get it?"

Henry Kovalick looked a little embarrassed. "The papers seem to be missing," he said.

"I'm not surprised. Do you suppose *la belle* Schellenberg knows she owns this?"

"I suppose so. Really have no idea. We may have a little fun finding out. Henry, you better cover it up," Bobby said.

Then they came to Andrea di Guisto. Or Guisto di Andrea. It was typical of its genre, late fifteenth-century Florentine, the inevitable Madonna and Child flanked by a couple of obsequious angels. To the surprise of all present, Rupert was definitely and visibly excited by it.

Frank Rogerson registered incredulity and said, "You don't really think it's good, do you?"

"No, it's not good at all," Rupert replied without taking his eye from the magnifying glass. "All the experts from Vasari to Berenson agree this mysterious character never painted anything good. It's just about the only thing they do agree on so far as he's concerned. I'd like it on the table please. What do the files tell us? You have the provenance, Henry?"

"Afraid there's not much to go on, Mr. Conway. We've not found any bill of sale. No trace of where or when he bought it. Here's a file I put together myself. An extract from Colnaghi's Dictionary of Florentine Painters, the nineteen twenty-eight edition. A number of items there are close, but nothing exactly fits. Same with Vasari, this is 1558, the sec-

ond Florentine
records to wor
missed him, as y

"Had it X-ra

Henry put an
turned it on. Th
neath, nor of any

"Let's have it l

He spent anotl
vas with magnify
right," he said. "P
Gozzoli. Brushwo
woolly, no vigour i

Rupert stood ba

"I'm prepared to

Nobody said ar
moment of ominou:
ing some kind of
what's eating you?"

The problem was
volved. He was clear

"We have an auth
it just doesn't seem r
make of it."

"Let's have a loo
taken an unaccustome

With an apologetic
single sheet of paper.
game," he said.

Rupert read the impi
the top. "Duveen Broth
Avenue, New York City
May 23, 1939, and the
was "Joseph Duveen."

"Well, well, well," Ru

unusual docu
quaintly put
Someone wan'
self was inter
drea."

"Correction
more accurat
berg to believ

"Point take
There coul
of the letter
House of Du
donna and (
genuine worl
Renaissance
sold it to a g

"This is c
have a perfe
beyond its c
the trouble
provenance
ounce of rea

Bobby s
dence Sche
edge. He ju
sive enough

"Well, th
sive than D

Bobby a
the paintin

Without
lievable le
doubt at a

For th
slightly sc

48

lunatic solemnly asks us to believe that Duveens ever handled this picture. They wouldn't have had it in the gents lavatory!" He looked at it again quizzically and added, "Even if they had, Joe would have put Knoedler's name on it. It just screams at you, doesn't it?"

There was another long pause, then Henry's plump secretary opened her mouth for the first time and said very tentatively, "Didn't Lord Duveen die in nineteen thirty-nine?"

There was a pregnant hush but only one thing to say, and in his best Rex Harrison manner Rupert said it.

"By George she's got it! Bobby, you must have Sam Behrman's book on Duveen in your library?"

Jenny picked up the telephone by her elbow and issued a terse instruction to somebody. There were minutes of frustrated silence while Rupert paced up and down the room to get control of his excitement. Could he possibly be wrong after all? Of course he could, and he had sufficient vanity to hate making a fool of himself. Besides, this picture meant much more to him than vanity.

A young man was ushered in and handed the desired volume to Jenny. Rupert sat down with a bump.

"Right at the very end," he said impatiently. "Must be about the second to last page. Blast! I can just see it . . ."

Jenny flipped over the pages and then said, "Would this be what you want?" She read, "On seventeen May nineteen thirty-nine"—and before she could get the next word out Rupert almost shouted—" 'Duveen sailed for what he called home!' Of course, that's the giveaway. On the twenty-third of May Joe Duveen wasn't signing letters in New York, he was dying in his bed at Claridges. Right?"

Everyone looked relieved. For a moment. On reflection it was interesting, but it didn't really get them much further.

Rupert held the offending sheet up to the light, his expression a study in disbelief.

"It's expensive, certainly. But too flashy. Duveen was spectacular, never flashy. This is the sort of paper a high-class tart might use," he said feelingly, and quickly added, "and don't ask me how I know." He turned to Henry again and asked, "Where did Schellenberg buy most of his paintings?"

"Oh, very scattered. New York, Chicago, Philadelphia. Bought a lot in Europe, London, Rome, Paris. Quite a bit in Paris."

"Any particular dealer?"

"Not that I've noticed from the papers. He just shopped around as far as I can make out."

Rupert held the paper up to the light to study the watermark. "Any idea what this watermark is?"

Henry had the answer ready. "We've had the FBI check it for us. They have no trace of it on their records."

"Which would support my guess that it isn't American. European, almost certainly. Of course, it's quite possible Duveen bought his stationery in Europe. But not this. Bobby, let me take this back with me, will you? There is an outfit in Basle called the Criminal Techniques Department, Public Prosecutor's Office; they have catalogued just about every watermark since King Tut. They'll trace it for us."

Bobby replied, "Certainly, if you wish. But is it

really necessary? You've already declared the painting is genuine. I wish I knew how you could be so sure?"

"Oh, of course. I'd nearly forgotten." Rupert reached out for his attaché case lying on the table and opened it, taking out a large envelope of very old, yellowing photographs. He thumbed through them rapidly and handed one across the table. "From the Uffizi in Florence. They have the best collection on Italian paintings that exists anywhere. Bit dog-eared now, I'm afraid, but if you examine it carefully I think you'll be convinced it's the same picture all right."

Everyone gathered round to have a close look. No one wanted to argue the toss.

Bobby said, "Rupert, that really was damn cute. Mind telling us how you did it?"

"Don't forget, I used to be in the detective business," he said, without any feeling of false modesty. "You see I came armed with the photographs. There are only six paintings generally agreed to be by this character, and five of them I can account for. That narrowed the field a bit. There is one in Paris, two in Pennsylvania, funnily enough. Sold two of them myself in Geneva a few years ago. I've been looking for this particular exhibit since nineteen forty-five. It was on one of my lists when I was tracking down Nazi art loot after the war. That's why I'm so interested to trace the writer who forged Duveen's signature."

"You really do know all about it then?"

"Yes indeed I do. In March nineteen forty-five the painting was stolen by a unit of SS troops attached to the Twenty-sixth Panzer Division of the Wehrmacht. The soldiers retreated back to Germany, as they were ordered to after we broke through the Gothic Line. The SS thugs lingered long enough to sack anything that took their fancy. This was taken from the Convent of the Grey Nuns at San Leonardo di Monte."

"Where's that?" somebody asked.

"In the Tyrol, just a bit south of the Brenner Pass," Rupert replied.

Chapter 4

Rupert spent the whole of Tuesday locked in the gallery with Henry Kovalick and Jenny going through the catalogue mock-up picture by picture and line by line. They checked names, dates, places, every item of provenance available. Every scrap of paper was checked and double-checked by Henry. Every note and comment for eventual publication was drafted and redrafted by Rupert, after which Jenny typed it. Then he redrafted it again and she retyped it. They worked right through until seven o'clock when Rupert and Henry retired exhausted. Jenny returned to her own office on the third floor where she spent the next three hours with a team of girls making clean copies, photocopying and collating the final documents for presentation at next morning's conference with the owner.

Mary Schellenberg lived up to all the advance publicity. She arrived Wednesday morning exactly on the stroke of nine. From the moment her stately figure swept into the room she dominated everybody within range without once making any apparent effort to do so. Not that she was aggressive—she clearly never felt any need to be. In her early seventies, she was big, handsome and elegant, and what the French call "formidable." Though she never even mentioned money, she was completely sure of her place in the world and her ability to do anything she set her mind to. Her hair was thick, white, and topped by a black silk hat held in place by a diamond pin. Her make-up was everything that chic required without being a whit too much. Her dress was black, noticeably expensive without a hint of ostentation. She wore pearl earrings and a two-strand pearl necklace. She had one diamond solitaire on the third finger of her right hand. At least five carats, Rupert observed. He thought her face showed great strength, but not a trace of anything so unrefined as toughness. It was not a hard face, though the midnight-blue eyes had a spark in them like late-afternoon sun flashing off the cowling of a jet engine at 30,000 feet.

Her greetings were everything that politeness required and no more. She knew perfectly well who Rupert was and why he was there. She had heard from Bobby Walker the princely fee he had demanded for his services. She had unhesitatingly agreed to it, her only comment having been, "You pay half of it." When introduced to "Rupert Conway, from Vienna," she shook hands with a grip as firm as his and registered the same degree of interest as if they had said, "Bill Schultz from Wichita Falls."

Bobby escorted her to a seat on his right at the big table. He was too good a judge of human character to enquire whether she had had a good flight, or what was the weather like back in Wisconsin. Her quiet air of being in total command awed even Rupert. He went through the entire meeting without once venturing to produce his pipe. Possibly she even liked men who smoked pipes, but he would take his time finding out. He knew plenty of grand ladies in Europe, but she was something new to him. He thought her fascinating.

She listened intently while Bobby explained in detail what the work of the last two days had achieved. She went through Rupert's catalogue notes item by item, asking a few pertinent questions, and accepted all Rupert's answers without comment. She actually allowed herself just the breath of a smile of approval when told they had reduced the difficult cases down to two. Very delicately Bobby introduced the matter of the nude which claimed to have originated in "the school of Rubens." Rupert recited only the essential facts which made the attribution impossible.

All she said was, "Let's see it."

Henry Kovalick, wearing his most cadaverous smile, removed the black velvet sheet draped over it. She was clearly well aware that the men were watching her, not the picture.

"Awful," she said. "How would you describe it, young man?" she demanded of Rupert. It seemed she addressed every male under seventy as "young man."

"Decadent," was the only word he uttered.

"Of course," she said. "You're sure it is of no value?"

She seemed to prefer this staccato style of conversation.

"Not to you, Miss Schellenberg."

She sat in silence for a moment evaluating that.

57

Bobby asked, hesitantly, "May we sell it privately?"

"Certainly not, young man," she said. She had obviously made up her own mind what should be done. "Burn it."

Jenny made a note, Henry re-covered the offending vulgarity, and Bobby introduced the second problem.

The Andrea di Guisto panel was placed on the easel for her inspection, and Rupert came straight in with a question.

"Miss Schellenberg, I wonder if you have any idea where your brother bought this?"

"None at all."

That avenue led nowhere.

Bobby explained about the unsatisfactory provenance, which was passed for her inspection, and stated simply that Rupert declared it had been stolen. A sudden tautening of the skin around the eyes showed she resented the implication that her brother dealt in stolen property.

"Walter was one of the most objectionable men I have ever known," she said firmly, "but he was not a crook."

Rupert was undecided whether he had been slapped or not.

"No, of course not. I had not meant to imply that, Miss Schellenberg. I'm sorry. I have no idea how your brother acquired it. The fake provenance contains a few clues. With your permission I would like to investigate them." He paused a moment and took her slight nod as approval. "I will report to you, of course, as quickly as possible. In the meantime, the catalogue can be set up." He changed pace and tone.

"What I really want to convey is that the panel has very little artistic merit. It won't fetch more than two or three thousand dollars. Its only real value is to its rightful owners."

"I am its rightful owner," was her terse reply.

Ouch, Rupert thought, and cursed himself for being so clumsy. Bobby kept his eyes on the floor.

"Yes indeed. I apologize. I chose the word carelessly." That probably was not a good word to use in her presence either. This remarkable woman was getting him flustered, and it was a phenomenon he wasn't used to. Trying to win back a little ground he added, "Since the Statute of Limitations on wartime loot ran out on the first of January nineteen seventy-six, your claim is unchallengable in any court. But . . . as Bobby told you, I happen to know its history. I have been looking for it for many years. Not for myself, I assure you. If I could prove to you that it was stolen from the Grey Nuns of San Leonardo in nineteen forty-five . . . well . . . would you allow me to return it to them?"

He had burned all his boats now.

There was another long silence around the table. The response, when it came, was even more devastating than anyone had feared.

"Certainly not, young man," she said. The words dropped with a cold, metallic clink like a surgeon's scalpel being tossed into a steel tray. And just as bloody, Rupert thought.

She appeared oblivious to the almost audible groan that vibrated round the room. "She's far too intelligent to be so insensitive," Rupert was thinking. "She does it on purpose. I wonder why?"

Just as laconically, she added, "I have no doubt

you could prove to me it was stolen from the Pope if you put your mind to it."

It was one of those ambivalent remarks that leave the person so addressed uncomfortably wondering whether it was meant as a compliment or an insult. Rupert found himself becoming more fascinated than ever by this formidable woman. But not nearly so amused. He felt rather like a schoolboy who had just been verbally slapped with that ghastly old stinger, "Boy, wipe that smirk off your face!" Doing business with Mary Schellenberg was a deadly serious affair. Rupert had no doubt that she had seized the opportunity to put him at a disadvantage because that was exactly where she wanted him.

But his spirits were resilient. That crack about the Pope did leave a chink open which, with a bit of luck, he might just be able to crawl through. Choosing his words this time with meticulous care and deliberation, he said contritely, "Miss Schellenberg, I'm sorry if I chose my words badly, but, please, understand that I have spent much of my life dealing with the tragedies arising from the spoils of war. I admit to strong feelings about these matters. May I rephrase my question?" Once again she said nothing and once again she left him with no choice but to assume her silence conveyed consent. "If I can prove to your satisfaction that the man who sold the Guisto panel to your brother knew it was stolen and how it was stolen, and if I can prove to your satisfaction where it was stolen from, and how this dealer came by it . . . if I could do all this, then would you let me give it back to the nuns?"

The midnight-blue eyes flickered, and Rupert watching them intently thought that a tiny ray of hope was about to emerge.

Then she said, "Well, young man, why don't you try it and see what happens?"

She gathered up her handbag, her gloves and her glasses and rose. They all stood up, and since she was aiming for the door Bobby escorted her to it. On her way across the room she bid everybody a polite, almost kindly, "good-bye." As she reached the door she turned back, and speaking directly to Rupert she switched the ray of hope down several watts, "But you haven't much time. If the sale can't start by the twenty-fifth of June, it's off."

Rupert smiled across the floor at her and said quickly, "Where can I get in touch with you?"

"I'm leaving for Europe on Saturday. I'll be moving around, but the Connaught in London will always find me."

They worked out a campaign over lunch. Henry would complete a list of every art dealer whose name appeared in Schellenberg's files plus all relevant information he could find, and he would get it into Rupert's hands before he left New York. Rupert would phone the Basle investigators first thing Friday morning from Paris and would get the "Duveen letter" sent to them by special courier the same day. It was agreed that if the dealer who had sold the Guisto to Schellenberg appeared to be in America, then Bobby would take charge of the proceedings; if in Europe, Rupert promised to drop everything to deal with it. Walker, of course, would pay all expenses.

Rupert phoned Malcolm Forbes' office to find that he was in Cape Town, so he left an enigmatic message mentioning Fabergé, which he hoped would catch Forbes' curiosity, and spent the afternoon at the Russian exhibition in the Metropolitan Museum. He still had time for an hour's sleep and a shower and shave, before making the pilgrimage down to Fifty-sixth Street to L'Aiglon. Guido excelled himself. For the first time Rupert was subtly glad that he had come to New York by himself. Jenny loved soft-shelled crabs.

Chapter 5

Horst awoke slowly, painfully, in a semi-darkened room with a gabled ceiling. His first awareness was that he was lying on a bed, somebody had taken his coat and boots off and placed a blanket over him. A pale shaft of sunshine was filtering through an intricate fret-work pattern in the shutters. His next awareness was that he ached from head to foot—especially his head. But he was conscious, and he remembered clearly the accident to the glider. That was reassuring; he probably had suffered a mild concussion, nothing worse. As he tried to discern his surroundings he made the alarming discovery that he was only seeing out of one eye. Very gently he moved his right hand to his face to investigate. One eye was heavily bandaged. He tried to blink, and while it hurt badly, he could discover a sliver of light along one edge of the bandage. So he wasn't blind either. The cut must be on the upper eyelid. And the right arm and hand worked normally. He remembered quite clearly falling through the tree.

He began to consider his situation. He hadn't bargained for this; it hurt, but he was tough. This was Mario's house. He had slept in this room before. Where was Mario? Not here, he hoped. A man came into the room, but it wasn't Mario. He was a big powerful man, and he was wearing the black robe of a priest. They were both quite still for a moment staring into each other's eyes. The priest did not smile; his expression was gentle, but stern.

Horst still ached too much to attempt movement, but there was nothing wrong with his speech.

"Who are you?" he said quite coherently.

"Father Bruno," he replied. Mario's brother. Horst had met him once or twice on previous visits. He wondered how much Father Bruno knew about him.

"Where's Mario?"

"At the moment we don't know."

"Don't know?"

The priest's expression hardened.

"No," he said, and there was anger in his strong Tyrolean voice. "He should have returned Thursday night, but he didn't." Horst had known that before he left Leipzig.

"Is Gabriella here?"

"Gabi is here. You will understand she does not welcome you in her house."

"Yes, I understand that. I'm sorry for her. Gabi's a good woman, but . . . Mario was a *brigatista* long before I met him."

The priest felt no need to comment. He said, "Do you feel able to stand?"

Horst braced both elbows and very gingerly dragged his reluctant body into a sitting position.

"How did I get here?" he enquired.

"I carried you."

Horst shifted his body a bit and rubbed the bruises on his head. "Thank you," he mumbled.

"It was no more than my Christian duty." He paused. "Get up and try to walk," Bruno said quietly.

Horst found the first few steps a little shaky and he had to grasp the bed-post for a moment, but he made it to the window and back with the priest's keen eyes studying him intently.

"Good, you couldn't have done that if anything had been broken. I'm not a qualified doctor, but I'm the closest thing there is around here for many kilometres. You'll find water in the bowl, your valise is on the floor there. Get yourself tidied up and come downstairs. Gabi will get you a meal, and we must arrange your departure." With that he was gone.

Horst sat on the edge of the bed to think for a moment. Gabi and the priest seeing him was a pity. Would that fracture his previous secrecy? No way of knowing. A sudden thought made him feel under his left armpit. The Makarov was still in its holster. He took it out and examined it. There were still seven rounds in it. The priest had removed his leather jacket. He couldn't have missed the gun. The idea of not removing another man's gun was heresy to Horst. Something to do with "thou shalt not steal," he supposed. It was no surprise to him that his valise had not even been opened, and the hundred thousand lira tucked in his shaving case was untouched. The keys of his Bologna apartments were there too. Then Paris, and . . .

By the time he had finished washing, and exchanged his heavy boots for the soft rubber-soled shoes that were part of his standard equipment, the

65

sun had fallen down the other side of the Alps and night swept into the valley with a rush. Horst didn't make any particular effort to walk downstairs silently, it was just part of his training. As he stood for a moment looking round the familiar little hall he was conscious that the kitchen door was open. What he found himself looking at was Father Bruno's cassock encircled by the white arms of his sister-in-law whose body was welded into his. Over the priest's left shoulder he could just see her brown curls. Her face was buried in his outsize chest and she was crying her heart out.

As Horst walked noisily into the kitchen and Gabriella's tear-reddened eyes caught his he felt miserably out of place and unwanted for the first time in years. To his own surprise he found himself mumbling, "I'm sorry, Gabriella." Though he didn't realize it, he was starting to react like a free man already. The humanity which may lie dormant for years can reassert itself at the most unexpected moments.

Without a word Gabriella turned to her cooking and the priest said, "Wine and glasses are on the table. I dare say you need it."

Horst filled a glass in silence and dropped into the nearest chair. The priest walked across the room, tossed a newspaper in Horst's lap and went out saying, "I'll be back in five minutes."

The paper was Friday's *Correria della Serra* and half-way down the front page was a story headlined, 3 TERRORISTS KILLED IN LATEST OUTRAGE. It was believed that at least two others had been wounded but escaped from the scene of a pitched battle with the *carabinieri* outside a bank in Turin. No names were given. Horst understood Gabriella's tears and

66

her silence very well. She had hated him from the first time he came to their isolated farm-house in San Jacopo. She had good reason to. She hated the fact that her husband was a terrorist, that he killed people and believed in killing people. What made her situation even more intolerable was that she passionately loved Mario; she longed for the children she could give him, and his return to teaching here in her native Tyrol. On more than one occasion when Horst had spent a night there his sleep had been disturbed by Gabi's sobs, sometimes her screaming at Mario, "You'll be killed! You'll be killed!" At the time it had merely irritated him. As far as he was concerned he had a duty to do. It was easy, then, to be totally immune to the pleading of hysterical women.

After a melancholy dinner during which the only words uttered were the priest saying grace, Father Bruno took Horst in his little Fiat and drove him all the way to Bolzano where he caught a train to Bologna.

Mario never returned. Four nights later Father Bruno, calling by to comfort Gabriella, found her lying battered in a pool of blood on the floor of her ransacked home. He rushed her to the nearest hospital, at Bressanone; all she was able to tell him was that two strangers came enquiring after Horst. They wouldn't believe she had no idea where he had gone. She died the next morning.

On the north side of the Alps the Provincial Police Praesidium at Innsbruck was in a state of more than usual animation. All day Sunday policemen and detectives had been scouring every metre of ground between Gries and the Brenner Pass frontier post. They had found the bullet from the Makarov embedded in a pine tree on the other side of the northbound traffic lane, and indications in the undergrowth near the lay-by which suggested that a human body had lain there the previous night. Presumably it was a live human body. The truck and the area around it were photographed from every possible angle, including from a helicopter, the lay-by was cordoned off and plainclothes officers patrolled the area.

On Monday every man who could be spared from the rest of the Tyrol Länder was drafted to a temporary headquarters established at Gries from where a manhunt was directed. The big meat truck was removed to the Praesidium compound in Innsbruck where the forensic experts went over it, inside and out, with immaculate care.

Since the murder of a German Communist driver in a German Communist-owned vehicle meant inevitable political problems, the wires between the Police Praesidium and the Ministry of the Interior in Vienna were humming. An Under Secretary telephoned a senior official at the GDR embassy to inform him of the incident and received, as he had expected, a noncommittal and disinterested reply. When to his astonishment, the official called back two hours later in a state of some agitation the Under Secretary thought it wise to inform his Minister personally. Fatal accidents, and even rare murders of East Germans were not unknown in neutral Austria. They always caused problems, but the chief problem usually was that the GDR authorities didn't want to know anything about them. From their point of view there was obviously something special about this one. The Minister, Otto Rosch, thought it prudent to speak to the Tyrol Police President himself and offer any assistance within his power. After some consultation the Police President said it might be helpful if he could borrow a senior officer with experience of dealing with "political" matters to join his team, and the Minister promised to find one. The choice eventually fell on the number-two man of the First Department, Security, in Vienna Praesidium, Hofrat Josef Liebmann. When Liebmann conferred with his colleague in Innsbruck by phone one of the most intriguing things he learned was that the meat truck had been found to contain a heavy canvas bag in which were rolled what appeared to be old and valuable Italian paintings. Before leaving by helicopter for Innsbruck Wednesday morning Liebmann had the inspiration to phone his good friend Rupert Conway who specialized in knowing about stolen paintings. He learned from Sandra Fleming that Conway was in New York but by happy chance would be in the vicinity of Innsbruck by Friday night.

Chapter 6

On Tuesday while Rupert was wrestling with the Schellenberg catalogue in New York, an attractive, smartly dressed woman in her middle thirties landed in East Berlin off the Aeroflot noon flight from Moscow. A chauffeur-driven black Volvo met her and drove direct to the ornate but dilapidated National Hotel.

As she got out of the car the chauffeur handed her a note which told her she had an appointment at the Russian embassy at five o'clock. Precisely at that time she walked the two blocks down Unter den Linden, that sad and colourless boulevard which for two hundred years had been one of the grandest in Europe, and presented herself at the main entrance of No. 63/65, the only building on it which still makes the slightest pretensions to grandeur. She presented her pass to the sentry on duty, an officer promptly appeared, and she was ushered directly to the office of His Excellency Comrade Pyotr Abrassimov, Russian Ambassador to the German Democratic Republic, and de facto ruler of that country. No mere run-of-the-mill diplomat, Abrassimov is a member of the Central Committee of the Communist Party of the Soviet Union.

Technically, historically and legally, since no peace treaty has ever been signed between the Second World War Allies and "Germany," all Berlin is still under Allied Occupation as laid down in the Yalta Agreement in 1945. Until that agreement is amended, no German has authority over anything without the approval of the four Allied Military Governors designated in the Agreement. In West Berlin the British, American and French generals still meet once every month to discuss local housekeeping and high politics, and still always keep an empty chair at the table for their Russian colleague should he wish to turn up. He is informed exactly where and when they meet. In fact, no Russian representative has attended these meetings since the great "Air Lift" of 1947-48 proved to the Kremlin that the Western Powers would never surrender their rights in the city without a fight. For thirty-two years the three Military Governors, whose writ is limited de facto to West Berlin, have managed to work in very nearly unbroken harmony with the democratically elected political leaders. The generals are backed by a three-power garrison that seldom amounts to more than ten or twelve thousand men. It is not the numbers, but the token of their presence that matters; everyone knows only too well that if they were to leave, the Russians would take over West Berlin within hours. The generals run the most popular and inconspicuous military occupation in history.

In East Berlin, the other side of the manned,

mined and booby-trapped wall, their Russian counterpart sits in solitary splendour by himself, but he is supported by never less than half a million Red Army troops and has delegated nothing: neither the civic nor the state governments' resident within his jurisdiction can take a bath without his permission. Abrassimov presides over what is probably the most iron-fisted "colonial occupation" since the Romans sacked Jerusalem.

The sophisticated lady from Moscow was provided by the Ambassador and his aides with a full briefing on the latest and, from the Russian point of view, most unwelcome developments in the underground war being waged by proxy against the legitimate government of Italy. She also received her travel plans and a new set of papers; passport, visas, identification and travellers cheques. Armed with these she flew next morning to Vienna, changed planes for Venice, and on arrival there took a taxi to Mestre where she boarded an afternoon train to Bologna. Her papers were, naturally, all in perfect order; the journey totally uneventful. Her new West German passport gave her name as Anna Liese Ulrich. It stated that she had been born in Munich on February 21, 1944, which was true.

Bologna was the logical starting point for her mission. The Italian Communists had "captured" Bologna, more or less peacefully, in the first postwar elections and have successfully hung on to control of it ever since. Although the police and the *carabinieri* manage to maintain some measure of what the rest of Italy understands as law and order, the political and administrative machine of Mayor Renato Zangheri is completely controlled by the Communist Party. Marxism is dead, but the Party machine remains the dominant vested interest. It is the Party who run the highly profitable import trade from East Germany; the Party which ensures that Communist plotters of all kinds can carry on their activities as free as possible from interference by the government in Rome. The true relationship between the Communist Party hierarchy in Bologna and the "Eurocommunists" of Enrico Berlinguer in Rome is the city's most closely guarded secret; the innumerable Russian and East German advisers, experts and technicians are not so highly visible as they were, but no one believes they have left.

At five minutes to five she left the station on foot, carrying only a leather satchel over her shoulder, and made her way to a respectable but dingy nineteenth-century apartment block just off the Via San Stefano, climbed four flights of stone stairs, took a key from her handbag and let herself into the apartment. She had never been there before, but she knew exactly where everything would be and that everything she would need would be where it should. Strange surroundings held few surprises for her. And no fears. Countless Central Europeans of her age group had been born in air raids, weaned amongst bomb-shattered buildings and nurtured in concentration camps. The day-to-day struggle for existence, the night-to-night struggle with fear, produced a generation in which only the tough survived.

She tossed off her hat and coat, walked across the small living room and opened the shutters. The flat overlooked the piazza ominously known as "Pilate's Court." She knew she had precisely ten minutes from that moment until the doorbell would ring.

Ten minutes were sufficient for a quick wash,

73

combing of her black hair, and renewal of her lipstick. The fawn and light-brown suede suit fitted her trim figure admirably, and the green silk scarf at her neck gave it exactly the degree of femininity she chose to exhibit. She opened the door without any sign of apprehension or excitement.

The man who entered was tall and handsome in a rawboned Slavic way; twenty years working with the diplomatic service had given him the polish his vocation required. They smiled at each other as old colleagues would anywhere; friendly, but without any personal commitment. She extended her hand and he took it and bent over it with just the slightest bow to her and to old-world courtesy.

"Welcome to Bologna, comrade," he said.

"Thank you, comrade," she replied in similarly even tones. "I take it security here is all it should be?" They spoke in Russian.

That is just the sort of line she would open with, he thought to himself; relevant, polite and ice-cold efficient. He assured her that it was. He had not welcomed the news of her imminent arrival. People sent from head offices to ask questions cause apprehension in any business—especially one that has not been going too well recently. He offered her a French cigarette which she accepted, and they sat down to talk. She came straight to the point: why she had been sent, the anxiety at headquarters in Moscow, and Abrassimov's fury in Berlin. Her tone and her phrasing, his close attention to her every word made their relationship quite clear; they were colleagues of equal rank in the KGB, professionals clinically discussing a difficult and dangerous problem.

An acute listener might have observed a touch of

deference on the man's part; he was the field man, responsible for important and delicate matters in his own sphere, and in the last few weeks his branch had not been able to report the kind of things the bosses in Moscow liked to read. The unforeseen hostility of the mass of the Italian working people to the murder of Aldo Moro, the almost violent repudiation of the Red Brigades by the Communist Trade Union leaders, had been bad enough; this latest blow, the inexplicable disappearance of the man in charge of operations, Horst Rheinberg, was why they had sent the highly intelligent, cosmopolitan and inscrutable Anna, the only woman ever to reach the rank of Assistant Director in the State Security Service.

When she had finished he said with genuine consideration, "As usual, my dear Anna, while you do not show it, you must be weary from your travels. I have had a little refreshment laid in for you. The choice, I fear, is limited; our Bolognese comrades tend to a vodka which was made for Caspian fishermen. Buying scotch is a bit too conspicuous here, but the Italian brandy is quite drinkable."

"With a little Pellegrino and some ice, please, Boris."

Her words indicated a perfectly natural and unselfconscious sophistication. Everyone in the service knew that Anna was part French; indeed the Gallic strain was an essential part of the intuitive flair which had carried her to the top rungs of the Soviet espionage organization. Her French mother had been found in a German concentration camp in Poland in 1945 and "liberated" by the avenging Red Army. Who, or of what nationality, her father had been was known neither to her mother nor anybody

75

else; she had been raped by so many soldiers of so many different armies so many times that life itself was very nearly crushed out of her. When the horror was finally over she had two inestimable blessings left to her; a baby girl of quite unusual intelligence and striking appearance, and an almost miraculous freedom from the virulent Asian syphilis which countless thousands of other girls either died from or carried with them like a putrid cross for the rest of their lives. Boris Valishnikov poured two brandies and Pellegrino, handed one to Anna, sat down again, and began to tell his side of the story.

"My first news of the incident was when our liaison officer at the GDR embassy reported to me Sunday night that the truck carrying Rheinberg to Bologna had not arrived. Their local men had already searched Rheinberg's flat, and found no sign of anyone having been there."

Anna interrupted, "Where should Rheinberg have been?"

"His usual routine was to go straight to an apartment he keeps in Bologna, meet with his own staff stationed there to get up to date on events, change to his Italian identity, and then go off to meet Alunni and his people wherever they happen to be operating."

"And where is that at present?"

"Trento, just north of Lake Garda. Their next target is in Milan. So then, Monday afternoon I received a signal from my colleague in Vienna. It seems the Austrian police had notified the GDR embassy there that an East German vehicle had been found parked along the highway near Innsbruck, the driver dead with a bullet through his chest, and a murder investigation was in hand. The usual courtesies would be extended; the embassy's cooperation was invited. The key point, of course, is that long-distance haulage trucks always carry two men in the cab. The Austrian police say that the second man is missing and the truck contained nothing but meat. Whether either or both statements are true we don't yet know. Our German comrades are adamant that the vehicle was not carrying munitions. There is going to be one hell of a row if they are lying."

"That is the information I was given by our people in Berlin," Anna commented. It was the first comforting remark Boris had heard for several days.

"Thank God for that!" he said. "And they are also certain that Rheinberg was in the vehicle when it left Germany, are they?"

"They are."

"From the reports that reach me, the Austrians must be working on the theory that the murderer was the driver's mate. Who was Rheinberg . . . who is missing."

"Or already in their hands," she added ominously.

Boris didn't like that idea at all.

"Why should he murder the driver? And why in Austria? Why should he disappear? Where is he?"

"You tell me, Boris. He was your man."

However gently she put it, and Anna could be as gentle as a lullaby when she chose to, the implied threat was unavoidable. A stark vision of the inhospitable forests of Siberia flashed across Boris Valishnikov's mind.

"Not quite, Anna. Not quite. Remember, please, my orders, up till now, have been to encourage and to assist; specifically not to command. Support of the Red Brigades is directly an East German responsibility. Comrade Abrassimov has ultimate control over them; I haven't."

He was correct, of course. Anna sipped her drink in silence, aware that the sharp, almost certainly inescapable claws of the problem were digging themselves deeper and deeper into Boris's mind. He tried another tack.

"Is it possible that, for some obscure reason of their own, the SSD ordered Rheinberg to kill the driver?"

"My dear Boris, they wouldn't dare. Nothing happens in the GDR without Abrassimov knowing about it. Bismarck never ruled the Germans with half so iron a hand as he does."

There was no hope of comfort in pursuing that line of thought. Equally, Anna had no desire to be other than helpful, so far.

"A country run by sergeants," she continued. "All the officers have been shot or run away."

"Yes, that is my own impression from working with them. I've never served there myself." He lit another cigarette, lit one for her, and stood for a moment gazing thoughtfully out of the window. Having never read the Bible, the implications that what he was looking at was called Pilate's Court were lost on him. He turned back to face her.

Unable any longer to curb completely the anxiety in his voice, he asked, "Are you empowered to change my orders, to put me in command of the operation?"

"No, I am not. I may be given such authority, but not yet." She shrugged her elegant shoulders and continued, "You know as well as I do that headquarters are having what they call 'an urgent policy review.' Comrade Brehznev's heart condition has not been improved by the Moro incident. They hadn't reported Rheinberg's disappearance to him when I left Moscow." Without the slightest change of tone or pace she put her imprint squarely on the thought that had been growing like a malignant tumour in Valishnikov's brain since Monday morning. She could spot a landmine in a daisy field as well as he could. And she understood the implications for his skin as well as he did.

"Rheinberg knew too much to be allowed to defect to the West, comrade. If the West ever learned the real truth about what we are doing here, Brehznev's détente gambit would be blown sky high."

If that happened his most likely destination was not a labour camp in Siberia, but the Lubianka prison and a firing squad. For a moment he tried to comfort himself with the thought that even if Rheinberg did defect, there was a strong chance the self-indulgent fools in Britain and America would not believe it. Blame it on the CIA was a tactic the KGB had used with complete success before. It might work again.

Anna was known amongst some of her most senior colleagues as "The Sphinx," a name given her by Boris Ponomarev, the number-one man in the Soviet subversive apparatus, himself. But even he never suspected just how completely sphinx-like she was. Her continued silence did nothing to help restore Boris's customary sang froid. She wasn't playing with him, she had simply made up her own mind long ago what the truth must be, and decided he had better come to the same conclusion by himself. For the past three years, Valishnikov had been in charge of the Rome Kommandatura, that top secret section in every Russian embassy which even the Ambassador was never allowed to enter—except in East Berlin. He knew only too well the Kremlin files contained many reports of his ideas, his plans. The brilliant idea of adopting the East Germans to play the role assigned to their Cuban stooges in Africa had originated in a report he had written. War by proxy had been a KGB specialty ever since the revolution; Lenin's essay on the subject was holy writ in the Kremlin. He, Boris Valishnikov, was one of its most skilled practitioners. There was no escape from those files.

He snuffed out his cigarette and drained his glass.

He stood up and gazed out of the window at the medieval skyline of Bologna's fortress towers and baroque domes.

"Has Rheinberg defected to the West?" he mused out loud, and answered his own question. "I don't know. I don't suppose we shall ever know. It is a risk none of us can afford to accept. So, there is only one thing to do."

Having made his decision restored his composure.

"I must return to Rome at once. I shall send a full report of our discussion to Moscow."

As he turned to leave he said, "Let me show you your kitchen."

She followed him. All the cupboards were well stocked with food. He went to the electric cooker and turned the control knob for the back burner.

"You will find this one is not working," he said and opened the door of the small oven underneath. "But, if you turn it to nine and then back to seven, you can lift out the bottom panel. In here." He pointed to a flat metal case beneath the panel. "It contains everything you will need to know; a complete duplicate of my own file."

"Nine and back to seven," she repeated.

"I shall call you in the morning. At ten minutes to nine. There is a phone with a scrambler button in your clothes closet. The municipal authorities in Bologna are most cooperative." He forced a chilly smile and was gone.

Anna spent the evening studying the file and decided there was no work for her in Bologna. As soon as she conferred with Boris in the morning she would head for the Tyrol. Her instinct told her that if there was going to be any progress—and there had better be—that was where the clues might be found.

Chapter 7

Rupert arrived at Innsbruck's modest airport late Friday afternoon, just beginning to realize how tired he was. He had had a satisfactory telephone conversation with an official of Criminal Techniques Department at the Basle offices of the Swiss Public Prosecutor, who assured him they would deal with "the Duveen letter" without delay; and arranged with Swissair's Paris manager to ensure its speedy delivery.

Until the following Tuesday or Wednesday at the earliest there was nothing he could do, and there was nothing he would rather do than surrender himself to the relaxation he sorely needed and the quiet delights of civilized friendship, which were characteristic of his old friends Count Anton Dohanyi, hereditary owner of Schloss Schönberg, and his charming Canadian-born wife, Sheila.

He was completely, but nevertheless pleasantly, taken aback when Tony Dohanyi informed him that his bosom pal Jo Liebmann was esconced in the Innsbruck Police Praesidium, where he and other senior police officers impatiently awaited Rupert's presence. Tony handed Rupert a small card and dropped him at the main entrance.

"Call me at that number when you're finished, it's only five minutes away."

"I'll get the police to run me out to Schönberg," he protested.

"No, no. Not necessary," Tony laughed. "That's my office at the Ski Bus Company. I've plenty of work to keep me busy."

Attention to detail, not an ancient title, is the secret of success these days. Probably was the case even when Tony's ancestor acquired the title; the Habsburg emperors were not in the habit of handing out honours unless they were earned.

Tired as he was Rupert was genuinely delighted to see Liebmann. They had been friends since 1946 when Rupert was occupying an office in a wing of Schönbrunn Palace from which he directed the British Army's art-looting investigations in Austria, and anywhere northward and eastward his Russian Army allies would let him travel. He had soon learned that meant almost anywhere he wanted to go, but only after they had carefully removed what he was looking for. Liebmann, gaunt and emaciated, had just been repatriated from a Russian prisoner of war camp, rejoined the Vienna Police, and been posted a one-star lieutenant to Criminal Investigation, where he worked closely with the Allied Military Government. He and Rupert quickly found that they were brothers in spirit; they were both deeply religious men, had the same love for fine art and music, and both smoked pipes with a gusto that at times tried some of their mutual friends to distraction. A meeting they both attended was no place for non-smokers. Liebmann, with the rank of Hofrat, roughly equivalent to a Brigadier General, and number-two man in "Security," was far from being emaciated these days, a giant of a man with the largest hands Rupert ever saw.

Their greetings were suitably hearty. Liebmann introduced Rupert to the Police President of the Tyrol Länder and the other officers in charge of the murder investigation. He emphasized that he was their guest and acting only in a consultant capacity. The President emphasized that the political complications of the case increased daily, and he was very happy to have the Herr Hofrat's ample shoulders help cope with them. Police work, not international etiquette and skullduggery, was his own specialty. He outlined the bare facts as they knew them so far.

The vehicle, as was to be expected, was covered with finger-prints. They had all been carefully photographed and copies given to the GDR embassy, but if things ran according to form they never expected to hear of them again. They had tried feeding them into the central computer in Vienna, but it spat everyone straight out again. There was nothing at all upon which to build a theory about where the missing murderer might have disappeared to. It seemed reasonable to suppose that he was an East German—and unlikely that he would tarry on Austrian soil one minute longer than he could help. He could have left the country in a dozen ways. André Bossard, Secretary General of Interpol at St. Cloud, and all frontier posts had been notified immediately, but they had nothing to go on. There were no witnesses and false passports were common currency amongst criminals these days. The Italian police were cooperating fully and were checking stolen-car records comparing them with their own. The man might have just walked back to Gries and got on a bus. To Italy . . . Switzerland. To anywhere. All the routine searches and enquiries were being pursued.

The only piece of hard evidence they had to work on was the murder bullet. From its markings, and the exceptionally powerful charge which would have been required to propel it through the body of a large man, two metal panels of the truck door, and then across the highway into a tree eighty-nine metres away, the armaments experts had deduced that it had almost certainly been fired from a nine-millimetre Makarov of the type recently put into manufacture, together with its parabellum ammunition, in East Germany. Such weapons, and such ammunition had so far been issued only to the army and certain sections of the police; they were difficult for civilians to acquire. They concluded, tentatively at this stage, that the man who had fired it would probably have been a member of some official body. From the unaccustomed interest the GDR embassy were taking in the case, and their delphic inability to offer any constructive assistance, they suspected he must be somebody important—possibly as SSD officer.

Any explanation of the presence of six apparently valuable paintings hidden in amongst the meat crates was, at this stage, pure conjecture. The President had been delighted with Liebmann's suggestion that the Herr Doktor might reveal something about the paintings which could assist the investigation.

Rupert had rapidly forgotten all about being tired. His first question was, "Do the GDR people know about the paintings?"

"To the best of our knowledge, no. They asked permission to examine the contents of the truck, which we granted, but I agreed with Hofrat Liebmann's suggestion that we keep the paintings to ourselves. At this stage, at any rate."

Liebmann interjected, "The Ministry aren't very happy about it, as you can imagine, but it seemed wiser . . . at least until we know more about them."

The paintings were brought in. They had been carefully fixed to pieces of plywood and were hung along the wall for Rupert's inspection. There was a long and pregnant silence while he took his time examining them. He asked for a magnifying glass and a powerful flashlight which were promptly produced. Other than occasional grunts of "interesting, interesting," and just once, "fascinating," it was nearly ten minutes before the discussion was resumed.

It was Rupert's turn to be delphic. He sat down again on the opposite side of the conference table where he was facing the six enigmatic exhibits and ponderously refilled and lit his pipe. Jo Liebmann, knowing Rupert's moods and habits so well, produced a prepacked meerschaum from a leather case, and smilingly followed suit. It was now nearly half-past five and several of the local team were becoming anxious to get home. It looked like a lonely week-end for their long-suffering wives. The helicopter pilot outside warmed up his engines, as if attempting to convey a message that even if Hofrat Liebmann was in no hurry to get home to Vienna, he was. Rupert puffed heavily, and finally spoke.

"Well, gentlemen, my first assessment is that the paintings are probably very valuable. At least, five out of the six. There are two with signatures which, from memory, I would guess were genuine: a Gerini and an Aretino. Not great painters, but good Renaissance craftsmen. The next is probably by a man called Bartolommeo Cristiani; it looks like his work. Same genre as the others. I don't recall seeing any of them before, so I really can't say any more without careful study. That means detailed examination, possibly X-ray, comparison with authenticated works by the same artists, which might be done with photographs, and, of course, one must attempt to trace their provenance. They all seem to be Florentine or Siennese artists of the fourteenth century— fortunately a well-documented period, and copies are usually not too difficult to detect. The one on the end is undoubtedly a modern copy of something. I can't be sure of what at the moment. Probably done in Rome about the turn of this century. The other two, I think I know. I have a feeling I've seen them before, but I must study my archives with great care, and make some enquiries, before I could be definite."

That left the assembled audience tantalizingly close to exactly where they were before. Only Jo Liebmann had an immediate question.

"Where do you think you might have seen them, Rupert?"

Rupert shot him a humourous, quizzical look and said, "At Frauenstein."

"Where's Frauenstein?" somebody asked.

"On the East German-Polish border," Rupert replied slowly through a rising cloud of blue-grey smoke. Jo Liebmann caught his eye with a look that said, "Don't overdo the arcane stuff, my friend." Rupert added, "Some years ago I had the opportunity to visit a warehouse, an old farm really, in East Germany, where a great deal of wartime loot was stored. I'd have to check my notes, of course, but I have a reasonably photographic memory for this kind of thing." He paused for a moment, and then continued, "My guess is that some, if not all of these paintings were looted by the German Army, probably from Florence or thereabouts, in nineteen forty-five, and have lain hidden ever since."

"At the farm near Frauenstein?" Jo hazarded optimistically.

"At the moment that's only a guess," Rupert said. "Do you want me to find out?" He was genuinely intrigued.

The Police President had no difficulty giving a direct answer to that one.

"Every item of detail is important in a murder investigation," he said.

"I was only there for an hour," Rupert said. "And . . . due to a little . . . ah . . . accident that took place during the time, it has not been possible for me to go back."

"But an officer of the East German Security Police would have had no difficulty going there as often as he wished?" Jo Liebmann speculated.

"That would seem a reasonable hypothesis," Rupert said. Liebmann's strong, expressive eyes stared straight into Rupert's thoughts, and he added, "Of course, I am always at the disposal of the Austrian police, but . . . all my records and equipment are in Vienna . . ."

Liebmann came straight back, "Just tell us what

you want, and we'll have it flown up here by helicopter straight away."

Rupert was on the verge of objecting that he'd planned a week of much needed rest when it suddenly crossed his mind that there was something, someone, in Vienna he would be only too happy to have flown up as soon as possible. "Perhaps, if I phoned my archivist . . ."

Detectives are trained to spot a clue however obscurely wrapped up, and Jo Liebmann was one of the best detectives in the business. It only took a few minutes to arrange that a police helicopter would pick up Sandra and whatever else Rupert considerered necessary to his research and deposit them in the grounds of Schloss Schönberg just as soon as they could be made ready.

It was after six o'clock when Count Dohanyi's white Porsche hurtled across the Europa bridge and Tony turned its low-slung snub nose up into the mountains. The narrow, twisting road first winds through three small villages, any one of which would be worth an historical novel: From the days of the Caesars they have been strategic strong points protecting the central north-south route between Italy and Middle Europe. In times of war the Franks, the Babenburgs and the Habsburgs, Cardinal Richelieu and Napoleon, have all fought for them as though they were the gateway to heaven. In times of peace they have all too often faded from men's minds—so far as to become derelict, ghost towns, as the young men drifted away to find a living in less hostile climes not buried half the year under ice and snow. These and similar small communities are the remnants of Europe's sole surviving mountain race, the Tyrolese, a people bred through centuries to a life that must be lived at the mercy of the overwhelming forces of nature, where the most ordinary vicissitudes of life allow no room for failure. Nature had shaped these people to its own service generations before strangers came from unheard of governments to tell them that their loyalties were the property of some unimaginable bodies called France or Italy, Switzerland or Germany. Today, since the modern world has surrendered to the forces of the great King Tourism, the people of these villages are more prosperous, healthier and better educated than ever before; but whether the person who services your car or brings your coffee is Tyrolese, Norwegian sailor or a Persian university student is something you have to find out for yourself.

They crossed over the fussy torrent of the Reutzbrunn, where the lights from the bridge formed a million shimmering sequins on the agitated surface of the grey-shadowed water, and passed the garish lights of advertisements and a space-age complex of brightly painted metal tubing that made up the base of the latest giant ski-lift operation. Then, as the road grew steeper and narrower, they were momentarily buried in a small pine wood, coming out on the other side to the very edge of a lake. The road now wound around the lake shore, and on the opposite side lay Schloss Schönberg. The generally accepted legend of the house is that its site had been chosen by one of Tony's ancestors, a Hungarian princess no less, whose husband had chanced upon the lake while accompanying Prince Eugene taking a short cut through the Alps to cut off Louis XIV's Army of Italy. If true, the lady unarguably had a keen eye for real estate. It was the only spot in the several thousand acres of rock and snow he had inherited where Tony Dohanyi—to the intense relief of his much-tried wife—did not want to build a hotel, a night club or a ski lift.

Schönberg is one of the most romantic private homes left in Europe, and the only piece of property in the Dohanyi enterprise that the travel writers are not encouraged to write about. Schönberg is "home"; it is dedicated to Sheila and their two daughters. Tony Dohanyi had not only been born of ancient and aristocratic lineage, he had had the even greater good fortune to inherit a shrewd and enquiring brain, which he worked unceasingly. The disasters which two world wars had visited on his parents had sharpened his natural instinct for survival, preferably first class, to a point little short of commercial genius. Though he looked like a caricature of the Austrian country gentlemen he was, and often amused or annoyed his friends by wearing the traditional Tyrolean grey-and-green-trimmed jahdar and tight knee breeches even in Vienna and Paris, he had been amongst the first to realize the potential popularity of skiing and turn it into an industry.

Long before the international boom got under way in the late 1950s he had been hard at work converting his vast and bankrupt inheritance into one of the most profitable tourist operations in the whole of the Austrian and Italian Tyrol. He was now expanding into France and Germany with equal determination and irrepressible panache. All through the lean post-war years Tony had worked, cajoling money out of sceptical bankers and exploring, frequently on skis, the farthest and most unlikely tracts of snow-bound mountainside acquired by his ancestors in order to cover them with ski runs, ski lifts, ski lodges, hotels, restaurants, service stations and souvenir stores.

Dinner that Friday night was casual, convivial and finished early. The host wanted an early night as he had to be up at six to get to a conference over breakfast at the top of Mount Patscherkofel on the other side of the valley. The Austrian authorities had recently installed some new solar-heating equipment in part of the complex they had built for the 1976 Olympic Games, and he was considering a similar plant in his newest Italian venture. He had arranged to inspect it in the company of the chief ski instructor from his Italian company, Nicci Corneto. Nicci and his glamorous wife, Carli, who had been Miss Italy not too many years ago, were then joining the week-end house party.

His sister and brother-in-law had driven over the mountains from Lyon that afternoon and needed no coaxing to an early bed. Cameron Chambois, cheerfully overweight with thick curly brown hair which belied his fifty-odd years, was France's leading authority on aviation law, and a director of Air France. From every aspect as Parisian as a man could be, he owed his distinguished first name to a Scottish mother. Louise, ten years younger than her husband, intelligent, vivacious and fluent in five languages, was a power in her own right amongst the arbiters of French literary taste. As Tony's only sister, she shared with him the restless curiosity of their Magyar ancestors and a keen interest in the family properties. She was a director of the controlling company of her brother's enterprises and kept a close eye on their marketing operations in Paris and London.

The other member of the house party was that indomitable old flirt, lifelong ornament of Viennese society, Princess Stefani zu Lauffenburg. Stefi had started lying about her age when she was underage and wanted to be thought overage, and it was a habit she never tried to break; somewhere in her middle thirties she just put the logic into reverse, and since she remained a stunningly beautiful woman nobody was going to argue. She had been a widow for thirty-two years, and it was sometimes noticeable that she was careful never to affirm nor deny the undying rumour that she had once been Archduke Franz Ferdinand's mistress. She was a sort of forty-second cousin of Rupert's and he adored her.

For everyone other than the host and hostess Saturday was a day of resting, reading and walking in Schönberg's spacious garden. Its very simplicity was one of its most striking features. Being presented by nature with a spectacle of monumental grandeur they had worked with it, not against it. The silver-blue of the lake, the myriad shades of green of the lawn and the trees, the lovely, soft creams and ochres of the facade of the house itself, and the white background of the mountains were subdued and humanized. The creation of a garden like Schönberg's is but a humble example of what nature and man can do together. To someone of Rupert's philosophic bent, a visit there always renewed his faith.

In the evening the food, the wine and the conversation were all unalloyed. Sheila Dohanyi's dinner parties reflected everything she liked, style without pomposity, excellence without extravagance, beauty without ostentation, and good conversation without rancour. Since she liked sharing her happiness with her friends, she entertained often; envy and quarrelsomeness were the only two total strangers to her table.

Nicci Corneto, like many other great Alpine skiers, was increasingly enthusiastic about hanggliding and had persuaded Tony to let him start a summer school. There were expensive and complex problems about insurance, and many underwriters didn't want to know about it. Cameron Chambois, who was also a director of an insurance company, felt obliged to defend his colleagues; he maintained the dangers were still too great and too unknown for a stable insurance market to develop yet.

Carli Corneto was at Padua University studying literature and history at the time of her sudden rise to fame and popular adulation. Ten years and two children later she continued to refine her intellect. She was currently working for her master's degree in classical studies by correspondence, and her figure was only just noticeably fuller. Like all women who combined good looks with the ability to talk well, she exerted a natural gravitational pull Rupert never attempted to resist.

Leaning on his arm as they went in to dinner Stefani croaked in his ear, "For Heaven's sake take your eyes out of that girl's bosom!"

Rupert laughed, "Afraid for my morals, Stefi?"

"Your morals are none of my business," the old lady replied tartly. "Her husband is bigger and younger than you are, my boy."

He was delighted to find himself sitting between Sheila and Carli at dinner. Both of them seemed genuinely interested in his views on art in general. He discussed the art of Peter Karl Fabergé with

94

Carli, and was joyfully surprised to find she knew all about the elephants in Queen Elizabeth's collection.

During the fish course Louise Chambois fulminated against the degradation of much modern American literature arguing that the glut of foul language, drug culture and pornography which emanated from across the Atlantic was gratuitous aid to the Communists in their compaign to persuade the Moslem world that America really was decadent. "Just look at Iran," she exclaimed. She firmly stated her own view that sex was beautiful but, unlike justice, should not be seen to be done. She was delighted by Rupert's quotation from such an unlikely source as Oscar Wilde that "The kingdom of pornography is so small you can travel it from end to end in twenty minutes."

"After all," he added, "there only are six words and incessant repetition becomes boring."

"What's the sixth one?" the spritely old Princess challenged him.

Rupert gave her an amused glance, thought for a moment, and said, "Pussy, Stefi, but it depends how you say it."

"Pussy?" she said. "That's not obscene, only vulgar."

"Vulgarity is a complex subject, difficult to define," Sheila put in.

"It's like garlic," Rupert said.

"What's it got to do with garlic?" Stefi demanded.

"Vulgarity is to life, my dear, what garlic is to good cooking; a touch here and there, handled with skill, is superb. Too much makes anything uneatable."

The chef's delicate touch with the garlic made the Tyrolean Saddle of Chamoix unquestionably superb.

Over the soufflé d'Armagnac Stefi berated Tony for appearing in the Palais Schwarzenburg in Vienna for dinner wearing his green jahdar and tight knee britches. Sheila looked amused, and Tony turned helplessly to his sister for support.

"He has to do it, Stefi," Louise said brightly.

"Has to? Why does he have to?" the old lady insisted. Tony grinned and said, "Better tell her, Louise. The secret will come out soon anyway when the company goes public."

"Well," said Louise, putting down her wine glass, "years ago, when we opened our first souvenir store, our publicity agent in Munich told us jahdar and lederhosen would be a 'big seller' to the tourists. He was absolutely right, but we had a lot of trouble getting the quality we wanted. So, I started a little factory of our own. We found a wonderful man called Karl Alder to run it, and he's done so well we now have five factories. Tony's our most successful salesman."

"Your father would have had apoplexy," Stefi snorted.

"You know the difference between rape and rapture, Stefi?" Rupert said.

She just gazed at him wide-eyed.

"Salesmanship," he said triumphantly.

With her usual caustic vivacity the old lady replied, "You don't improve with age, dear boy."

Around the fireplace in the drawing room Nicci Corneto returned to his current hobby horse, the problems of insurance cover for hang-gliders.

Cameron murmured his previous defence, but with little conviction.

"I'll bet you a bottle of chianti to a Coca-Cola," Nicci said, "that if the insurance people really studied the statistics of accidents, they'd find it was no worse than that of fixed-wing gliders, and they've been covering them for fifty years."

Rupert and Tony listened amused as Nicci's enthusiasm and experience continued to bear down on Cameron Chambois, who took it all in good heart.

"You get accidents in any sport," Nicci pressed. "Look at grand-prix racing. Motorcycles. Even football and what about boxing? The insurance companies have been covering gliders for years, and they have plenty of accidents. I saw a fellow crash only last week-end. And he was flying a Paul Macht Seven, one of the safest gliders ever built."

"Was he badly hurt?" Cameron asked lamely.

"Oh, I've no idea. We were two thousand metres away, up on the cliffs beyond San Jacopo. But we didn't have a single accident all day."

"What's a Paul Macht Seven, Nicci?" Tony asked.

"Well," Nicci rubbed his chin a moment, "Paul Macht is one of the finest Austrian designers in the game, and I guess, it's his seventh design that has gone into production."

"Can you really tell the make of a glider from that distance?" Tony said.

"Like anything else, one gets used to it. I've seen you spot a fault in a ski track from that distance."

Gazing out his bathroom window while shaving Sunday morning Rupert watched the gliders careening off the eastern tip of the Schlik a thousand metres above his head on the other side of the valley. It started him thinking, and he raised the subject again with Nicci when they met at the breakfast table.

"That glider accident you were talking about last night. You said it was an Austrian make?"

"That's right." Nicci helped himself to more bacon and eggs.

"And you were near San Jacopo, Italy?"

"That's right."

"Do you use many Austrian gliders in Italy?"

Nicci grinned. "No, not really. And they don't use many of ours. The business is too small. We're still in the stage where everybody wants to prove their own equipment is best."

In a thoughtful mood, Rupert wandered out into the garden and lit his pipe.

He and Tony, Sheila and Louise drove down to Mass in the little Catholic church in the village. Having one Jewish grandfather and the other a Welsh Methodist, Rupert was brought up in the Church of England, and from university days had been a one-man ecumenical movement. He always enjoyed the Roman rites, especially in places like the Tyrol where they were staunch traditionalists. But he had a hard time concentrating that morning.

As soon as they were back at the Schloss he phoned Jo Liebmann and told him what was on his mind.

"Assuming our missing murderer was an East German Security Service man, is it likely he would know anything about gliding?"

Jo pondered a moment and then said, "Yes, quite likely, I should think. The Germans were the first to develop paratrooping, you know. And the Russians keep them short on military equipment; still don't really trust them with the big stuff. We're grasping at straws, God knows, but I'll make some enquiries." There was a pause, and then he went on, "You know something, Rupert?"

"What's that?"

"You've just ruined my Sunday afternoon."

Chapter 8

Horst Rheinberg, now travelling on an Italian passport as Guiseppe Giancollo, spent most of Sunday,
May 21, wandering moodily around the Bois de
Boulogne. He had not anticipated that the art dealer
would be so hesitant. The flat payment offered for
accepting the paintings, tacitly understood to be
stolen property, was a mouldy fraction of what Horst
had anticipated. The dealer admitted frankly that
his offer was low, but "If *il signor* wants more? Well
then, we must have time." It would need time to
make a realistic valuation, time to make a few enquiries, explore the market, see who might be interested.

Horst was sorely tempted to bully, even attempt to
blackmail the frail little man with the thick glasses,
cigarette-strained fingers and the twitching thin lips.
Two things made that impossible, at least for the
present. The first was that so far he had still not
been able to think out any way of using the knowledge gleaned from the SSD files without blowing his

cover. Other officers over many years had had access to those files, and it was always within the bounds of possibility that someone else might have found the information in them intriguing. The second obstacle was a young, pale-faced man called Louis who hovered over the dealer's shoulder like a predatory bird and never left them alone throughout the negotiation.

If that wasn't enough to make a man feel moody, he was still far from recovered from his accident. He wondered if he had cracked his skull when he hit that tree. Father Bruno had thought not, but then Father Bruno was not a qualified doctor. His head ached almost unceasingly, and the deep cut above his right eye was slow to close, necessitating frequent changes of bandage. Still, here he was. Safely in Paris, and so far no one had asked any awkward questions. He knew very well that by now his recent employers must be frantically looking for him, but they had no reason to look in France. He was certain no one but Heinrich had ever got a smell of the picture game, and wherever Heinrich might be, he wasn't giving interviews to the SSD. He was glad, as he always had been, that he had no family or close friends to worry about. It didn't pay to have friends in the security business as practised by Communist governments. To them "security" embraced the whole of life, and they took it all too deadly seriously. The only people they could haul in for questioning were some of his fellow SSD officers. He didn't envy his Division Commander the grilling they would be putting him through by now. He had never liked the man, but he held no grudge. To his surprise he found himself almost feeling sorry for him. They might even shoot him—Horst had never thought of that before. A week ago his reaction would have been "all in a day's work." Somehow, sitting here in a park in Paris, watching people whose whole approach to life was so obviously relaxed, cracks were beginning to appear in his iceberg of cynicism. It did not make him feel any more comfortable.

A group of children just in front of him were rushing around flapping their arms, pretending they were airplanes. Four girls, two of them quite pretty, rode by on the bridle path laughing at some private joke. Children and young girls at any rate were very much the same the world over. He couldn't think of any personal hostages to fortune he had left behind. Mario's wife? She had no reason to like him. He felt genuinely sorry for her, but he reassured himself she was too sensible a girl to blame him for Mario's disappearance. She wouldn't want to get involved in more trouble. With a little bit of luck Mario may not have been killed; the paper hadn't actually given any names. The priest only knew that he, Horst, had gone to Bologna. They would look there anyway. They wouldn't find anything.

The trip to Bologna he would not soon forget. The journey had been nightmarish. The ache in his head, the weakness from loss of blood, and the ceaseless screams and tears of three children combined to make sleep out of the question. The train was packed, so there was no point trying to find another seat. The poor, sickly-looking girl who appeared to be the mother of the three fledgling Attilas was incapable of controlling them; if they weren't fighting or shrieking, they were noisily sucking oranges and throwing the sticky, half-chewed skins at each other. Naturally, none of them had very good aim. Finally, when the smaller of the two boys urinated on his sister's doll, Horst staggered to his feet suffering acute nausea and spent the rest of a miserable night in the corridor slumped unhappily against the lavatory door. He arrived in Bologna just after dawn in a state of complete exhaustion.

It was Tuesday night before he found the strength to organize his luggage and drag himself back to the railway station to board a train for Milan. There he got a few hours more rest in a working men's hostel run by a Catholic laymen's society, after which he went to a travel agency in the Piazza della Scala and bought a railway ticket to Barcelona where he had no intention of going. Armed with an Italian passport and a ticket to Spain he felt reasonably confident that the frontier authorities at Mentone would not question his cover story.

The Immigration Inspector gave his passport a perfunctory glance and said, "Where are you going?"

"Spain."

"Have a nice trip."

That puzzled Horst a bit. It was a phrase he had never met before.

Customs presented a slightly greater hazard. The long tubular metal case invited enquiry.

"What's in there?"

"Fishing rods."

The Customs officer's eyes took on a rare glow of friendliness.

"Fishing rods?" His tone of voice was frankly envious. "Where you going?"

"Segre. Spanish Pyrenees."

"Best rough fishing in Europe. North of Lerida."

"That's right."

Horst left the train at Nice, destroyed the ticket to Barcelona, and caught the first train to Paris arriving at the Gare de Lyon late Thursday night. He found a small back room in a seedy little hotel just off the Quai de Bercy.

He slept half-way through Friday morning. By the time he had made himself look reasonably presentable, debated for the seventh consecutive day and for the seventh time decided he would continue to let his beard grow, and swallowed sufficient steaming black coffee to stimulate his wearied nervous system, it was after eleven o'clock. He had long ago considered which three pictures he would present for his opening ploy with the dealer, but it took another half hour to extract carefully one of the larger canvases from its protective plastic roll inside the fishing rod case, and two smaller ones from the lining of a suitcase. By the time he found the dealer's shop in the Boulevard des Capucines, it was already closed for lunch.

He went into the first three banks he found and changed all his lira into francs. Then he had a beer and an *omelette aux fines herbes* at a nearby bistro and went back with his wares at two o'clock. Most of the afternoon had been spent in wrangling and disappointment; his few moments of satisfaction only coming when he had a chance to quote the time, place and exact price at which some painting comparable to the one under consideration had most recently been sold at auction. His knowledge gained from the Italian newspapers served some useful purpose, if only to impress them that he knew what he was selling. But, of course, they always had an answer. "Ah, yes, signor, but that one had for

104

many years been in the family of Madame la Duchesse de la Quelquechose"; or, "Oh, but the reason the price was so high that day was because there were two gentlemen from Houston, Texas, in the auction room at the same time." While they busied themselves taking endless photographs and making notes, Horst had ample time to reflect on the insoluble mystery of the art world—as of so many others—what is value?

In the end he left them on reasonably good terms and with reasonable confidence that satisfactory business could be done, given time and patience. The thin-lipped proprietor acknowledged the paintings were indeed of fine quality, and was frank enough to express his pleasure upon being told that there were more where these came from. He would have greatly preferred that the signor would leave these three in his care while they made investigations, but he understood the signor's caution. Something could be done from the notes and photographs they had made. By this time Horst was seriously reconsidering his own ideas about how he should proceed. If he could just get some reliable information on the state of the market in Rio or Buenos Aires, might it not be wiser at this stage to sell only enough to finance getting there? Strange, in all the time he had been planning this whole operation that thought had never crossed his mind before. He reflected that his time spent in Italy should have opened his eyes to such a contingency. But it hadn't. He was just beginning to realize that the real difference between the West and the East was not simply its vastly higher living standards; but more fundamental; it was the bewildering array of choices which confronted one nearly every hour of the day. Marxist teaching did not equip one to deal with such problems.

So, now, Sunday afternoon, he was a free man, alone in a brand new world; his plans a bit frayed here and there but essentially intact, and with the hope that the next decisive step might be taken successfully by about Tuesday or Wednesday. With luck. He was even feeling a bit rested, and the stubble on his chin had now grown enough to begin to look like a real beard. If only his head would stop aching, and the gash over his eye would close. He decided it was time he took the risk of seeking medical advice. He walked across the Boulevard Suchet and went down into the Metro. Half an hour later while waiting in the Out Patients Department at the Hôpital St. Vincent de Paul he fainted. When he came to he was lying in bed with half his hair shaved off and eighteen stitches in his forehead. A smiling young doctor told him he would have to stay there at least three or four days.

After a long telephone conversation with Boris Valishnikov on Wednesday morning the seventeenth, Anna informed him she planned to fly to Milan immediately where she wanted to see both their own and the East German field officers who were working on the case of Horst Rheinberg's ominous disappearance. She confirmed she had all the names and addresses she would need; she had memorized them and returned everything to the file in its hiding place in the oven. Everything except the photograph of Rheinberg. Boris undertook to have the German officer in Milan informed of her arrival and would be there himself before nightfall.

Comfortably installed in the Piedmont Imperiale Hotel late that afternoon Anna received a visit from a very uncomfortable and worried-looking German agent called Klaus Bach. He was tall, thin with large rabbit teeth and didn't look anything like a Secret Police officer. Berlin had sent him to pick up the pieces. They were sure Rheinberg was in Italy. Bach had five of the most experienced gunmen in the SSD in his team, with orders to shoot on sight, no questions asked. He had been working eighteen hours a day since he arrived Tuesday morning, making contact with every Red Brigade member whose name appeared in Rheinberg's reports. He was too obviously tearing himself into shreds to impress the important lady from Moscow. Her principle impressions, unspoken, were not what he hoped they were. It was painfully obvious he spoke not a word of Italian, and while he appeared to know the files by heart, he knew nothing about Italy. More sergeants, she thought to herself. It was clear to her that whether he liked it or not, Valishnikov would have to take command.

Bach reported that he had just returned from Trento where he had seen Alunni in one of his numerous hideouts, in the students' quarters at the university. He placed great importance on this historic meeting and his own immense cleverness in having been able to arrange it, but it turned out that Alunni was just as surprised and puzzled by Rheinberg's disappearance as they were. The only hard information he had elicited was that the *brigatista* member who had been Rheinberg's regular liaison man was one Mario Lugano. Alunni told him that Lugano's bullet-ridden body was at that moment lying in the police morgue in Milan. Bach had despatched two of his best men to Lugano's home in the Tyrol to see if they could turn up anything there that might be useful.

Valishnikov arrived just before midnight, but Anna was already asleep. They spent all day Thursday together in Trento conferring with Alunni, but it was a frustrating and fruitless pastime. He obviously knew nothing of Rheinberg's movements, and cared less. All he wanted to talk about was guns and ammunition. The only thing they did achieve was to impress on Alunni that the price of greater assistance was Rheinberg's blood. He agreed to inform the whole Red Brigade network throughout Italy that Rheinberg was a wanted man and there would be a large reward for whoever could find and kill him.

When they returned to the Piedmont, Bach was waiting for them. He was nervous that they might have dug something out of Alunni where he had failed, and was unable to hide his relief when he heard they hadn't. With his usual mixture of self-importance and congratulation, he informed them that the two men he had sent to the Tyrol had "interviewed" Lugano's wife and acquired the important information that Rheinberg had been there on Sunday. She had not spoken to him. She had no idea where he had gone.

There was still nothing in any news bulletin about a major defection to the West, but that wasn't conclusive; neither side publicized such matters until it suited them. At least they now knew Rheinberg had been in Italy on Sunday. The Red Brigade was informed by Bach's people and urged to step up their manhunt. It was not difficult to convey to these zealots that it was primarily their own heads which were betrayed, their foreign friends merely wanted to help "in the interests of working-class solidarity and world peace." Both Moscow and the *brigatistas* agreed, for the moment at any rate, that one of the greatest enemies of both the working class and world peace was newfangled Italian "Eurocommunism." Three more Germans and two more Russians arrived in town to reinforce the team.

The Friday afternoon paper announced on the front page that Gabriella Lugano, wife of a notorious Red Brigade gunman, had died of head injuries in hospital. The *carabinieri* were treating it as murder.

"Stupid, clumsy brutes!" Anna said vehemently, to herself, in the privacy of her bedroom. Increasingly, there were moments when the mindless brutality of her colleagues cracked even her phlegmatic fatalism.

For the next four days nothing happened at all. All roads led to nowhere. Their watch-dogs covering main ports of entry and exit—Milan, Rome, Venice, and Genoa—had all drawn blanks. No one in Bologna had seen Rheinberg. His flat was exhaustively searched with no result. It was not until late the following Wednesday afternoon that a desk officer at SSD headquarters in the Frankfurteralle, Berlin, had the bright idea that there just might be some connection between the Rheinberg disappearance and a routine report on his desk mentioning an unknown Italian attempting to sell valuable paintings to the usual dealer they kept an eye on in Paris. He asked his superior for permission to study Rheinberg's confidential file. On Thursday morning it arrived on his desk. As he had presumed, Rheinberg spoke fluent Italian. Two hours and sixty-seven pages later he found a report in the file indicating that during his two-year stint in Criminal Records Rheinberg had worked on cases dealing with refugees smuggling works of art out of the Democratic Republic. He took the information to his superior, who thought it important enough to report to the General. The General talked to President Honiker's office, and early that evening it landed up on Abrassimov's desk. Coded cables started flying back and forth between East Berlin and the Russian Consulate in Milan.

Anna, Valishnikov and Bach were in continuous conference in the Consulate. At ten to eight it was decided that Valishnikov would remain in charge of operations in Italy while Anna and Bach proceeded at once to Paris. Abrassimov would inform the Russian embassy in Paris and put the full weight of his authority behind them. They dashed down to the waiting car and were whisked back to the hotel. The reception clerk informed them there was an Alitalia flight to Paris at nine o'clock. If they hurried they could just make it. The Consulate's Fiat sedan sped them to the airport in under fifteen minutes where they drove straight into a morass of confusion and struggling people: Just fifteen minutes before, the ground staff had walked out on strike. All flights were cancelled. They might fly tomorrow. They might not. Nobody knew. Anna knew very well what would happen if the ground staff, or anybody else for that matter, at Moscow airport ever dared try such a silly trick. However, once they had "socialism," Italian workers would undoubtedly behave better. Lenin had said so. Anna's private thoughts on some of the things Lenin had said were kept to herself.

110

icroscope and sorted lenses. Another police vehi-
e arrived from Innsbruck with the paintings. In his
rt sleeves, Rupert was in the middle of supervis-
their hanging in a way to take most advantage
he natural light when the phone rang. The farm
etary in the office next door asked if she should
the Herr Hofrat Liebmann through.

he two-hundred-and-fifty-pound Herr Hofrat
his genial, ebullient self.

upert," he said, "there are moments when I
er if you have a private wire to the Almighty
lf."

know a lot of influential people, Jo," he re-
heerfully. "You, for instance. What are we
about?" He sat down at Tony's desk and
to fill a pipe.

t wild shot of yours about the glider. You hit
et right on the snoot."

ve found our missing murderer?"

no. Not as quick as that. Frankly, I doubt if
will—there is no reason to think he will re-
ustria. But we have found out a bit about
rather a complicated story. Briefly, after
me I got in touch with a friend at *carabi-*
quarters in Rome. He arranged for their
le to search the area east of Brenner for
n-built glider we had reason to believe
re last Sunday. They put a signal out to
pter patrols, and sure enough, this morn-
und one. It was in a wood near an iso-
illage called San Jacopo, just where you
was a farm-house at the edge of the
rted and badly knocked about, blood all
e. They discovered it belonged to one
o. Nobody in the village wanted to talk

The Consulate car drove them all the way to
Nice. She made a phone call to a friend in Paris and
then caught a couple of hours' fitful sleep in the airport lounge. They took the first plane to Paris Friday morning. Bach was tired and bad tempered.
Anna never said a word to him during the entire trip
except, "Brandy and Pellegrino, with a little ice,
please."

Chapter 9

Sunday afternoon the week-end guests left Schloss Schönberg; Sheila and Tony drove off to Munich where he had a nine o'clock meeting Monday morning with his advertising agents. Rupert slept until nearly lunchtime Monday and never gave another thought to the masterpieces of Renaissance art locked in the vaults at either 720 Madison Avenue or the Police Praesidium in Innsbruck. After lunch he spent a couple of hours browsing through Schönberg's glorious rococo library; a rather large miniature of the National Library in the Hofburg at Vienna, complete with pot-bellied cherubs and buxom nymphs flying all over the ceiling. Somehow the nymphs reminded him of the beauteous Carli Corneto. Chancing on a leather-bound copy of Kenneth Snowman's encyclopædic book on the work of Karl Fabergé, he remembered something Carli had said at dinner Saturday night. She had told him as a positive fact that there were now more of the famous Imperial Easter eggs in the United States than

there were in Russia. It didn't matter very m checking up on such esoteric pieces of perfe less information always amused him. Carl Americans were winning by eleven to five dreamy idyll was shattered by the din of a landing in the meadow just outside the dows.

The pilot switched off his engines cious pastoral quiet was restored. For a onds. Then the chopper's side door sli Rupert watched expectantly the air shrieking and yelping of a fury as sound of his own voice. The next hurtled through the open door, half self in his lead; Sandra, franticall onto the other end of it very nearl him. Just as disaster seemed im arm of a policeman appeared i door and grasped the writhing her hand. Rupert opened the F ing into the garden and hurrie joy of the reunion was shared though in different fashions. S braced with the warmth wh cated love between two very ishes. Charlie expressed his round like a fly in a bott other of his hind legs aga came to. The policemen crates of various technica into Tony's farm office wing which had been tur

Sandra was busy files and photographs

about him, but the police already knew he had been killed in a Red Brigade shoot-out in Turin a couple of weeks ago. They radioed in their report, and when the computer swallowed the name Lugano, it threw up a suspected murder enquiry in Bressanone. Turned out to be this fellow's wife. She died in a hospital there on Friday morning. Cracked skull and multiple injuries."

"Good Lord! Our man had a really mean streak in him."

"That's what the Italians suspected, naturally. But it hasn't turned out that way. The woman had been admitted to hospital last Thursday night by Lugano's brother, a priest. So, they went to question him. He was pretty unhappy about the whole affair, but he didn't start to sing until they told him about his dead brother. Then he admitted he knew he was a *brigatista*, but not that he was dead. Said he had spent the week-end wrestling with his conscience. However, that news opened him up. He said he went to the farm Thursday evening seeking news of his brother, and found his sister-in-law unconscious on the floor. He swears that he revived her and rushed her to the hospital, but all she was able to tell him was that she had been beaten up by two men she had never seen before who came looking for the man in the glider."

"Did he know who he was?" Rupert interrupted.

"Just enough to tease us. He told the *carabinieri* all he knew was that the man was East German, and his brother called him 'Horst.' Seems he was some kind of liaison officer between the Red Brigades and their allies in East Germany."

Rupert's adrenalin count took a jolt.

"You said *East* Germany, Jo?"

"That's what the priest told them."

For the first time during the conversation Rupert put down his pipe and surprised both Jo and Sandra by breaking into a soft, unmusical, whistling sound. The political implications of this news were serious. Many people believed the Russians were secretly backing terrorists in Italy. Everyone knew the puppet government of East Germany took its orders from Moscow. Here was proof that the GDR government were allies of the notorious Red Brigades. And one of the individuals involved, possibly an officer in the army or the SSD, was wanted for murder in Austria. Neutral Austria. With the Russian Army sitting along her borders. None of that needed spelling out to a man of Jo Liebmann's intelligence.

"Jo," he said at length, "we're in deep, deep water."

"Who's we, Rupert?"

"I'm not sure I follow you?"

Jo said very slowly and deliberately, "I think you are way ahead of me, my friend. I'm an Austrian police officer investigating a murder—not a politician, remember?"

Jo could out-English the English as a master of the understatement. Rupert knew very well what he meant. Being half-Austrian himself, and having made his home there, it was a dichotomy he had learned to live with. Part of the price Austria had had to pay to get the Russians out in 1955 was a declaration of perpetual neutrality. It was enshrined as the very corner-stone of the young republic's constitution. Western-oriented in every way, NATO and all the entanglements of East-West confrontation were forbidden ground to Vienna. The awful irony of it all is that if war between the Communists

116

and the free democratic nations ever did break out, Austria would, once again, be the first victim. He lived there and loved it, but spiritually he was as Angelo-American as a man could be. Was he now in possession of a great international secret unknown to London and Washington? Suddenly, the thought that the Italians were part of NATO too flashed across his troubled horizon. That cleared his conscience. He heaved an audible sigh of relief.

Jo was a patient man, but he took the sigh as his cue.

"Want me to go on?" he asked.

"Of course, Jo. Of course. Sorry, my mind wandered."

"Well now. Father Lugano told our Italian colleagues that he visited his sister-in-law last Sunday—that's a week ago—and while he was there this Horst crashed the glider in the woods, right where they found it. The priest swore that all he did was to bandage the fella up a bit and put him on the train for Bologna. He says he hasn't seen hair nor hide of him since, and the *carabinieri* are inclined to believe him."

"I see. You said they found the glider. Does it tell us anything?"

"Quite a bit, actually. There were plenty of fingerprints in the cockpit, and presumably some of them were Horst's. As soon as we have them we'll compare them with those off the meat truck. If we get a match, that would tie up the connection all right. Good evidence in court, if it ever came to court. No trouble tracing the glider, of course. It bore Austrian registration and belonged to a man called Tolz who lives in a village near Brenner. Not an attractive type—criminal record, petty thieving, that sort of thing. He claims the German stole it from him, but that sounds unlikely. We're holding him for questioning at the moment. Put a watch on his house; never know who may turn up."

Rupert's mind was wandering back to NATO again, when Jo said, "How is your investigation on the paintings going?"

Rupert had completely forgotten about them.

"Only just starting. What do you want me to do?"

"Carry on if you will, Rupert. We'd still like to know everything about them we can. Going to be interesting to see if the East German embassy claim them."

"Certainly is. You've told them?"

"No, not yet. I'm not sure we will."

"I'd rather see them restored to their real owners, if I can trace them, Jo."

"That could probably be arranged."

Rupert put the phone down thinking Jo must be the world's biggest tight-rope walker. He lived on one. He was still brooding into a cloud of pipe smoke about the possible ramifications of the world of international subversion and intrigue he seemed to have stumbled into when the secretary came through again to say there was a call from Switzerland on the line. He hadn't even thought about Miss Schellenberg and her problems since last Friday. Fascinating though the riddle of the Andrea di Guisto might be, it was workaday stuff compared to the explosive possibilities resulting from the discovery of "the meat-truck collection."

The call was from the Criminal Techniques Bureau in Basle.

"We've traced this paper for you, Herr Conway," a cheerful voice reported. "It is French; made by a small specialty company. Leduc et Fils. The watermark was first registered in nineteen forty-nine."

"Thanks very much. Where do I find them?"

"You don't, I'm afraid. They used to be in Besançon but, like nearly all the small people in the paper trade, have been out of business for years."

"Damn. That's disappointing. What do you suggest?"

"Well, I wouldn't worry too much. Very few of these small people did direct selling; mostly went through wholesalers in those days. I don't know how Leduc operated—it was before my time—but there are people in the trade who could probably tell you."

"Where do I start?"

"Try Gaston Fonçier in Paris. They're one of the survivors. There is an old man called Adelbert who's been there since before the war. You'll find him cagey, but he knows as much about this fancy quality paper as we do. Sort of a hobby of his."

It would be difficult to deal with the cagey Monsieur Adelbert by long distance telephone, but he had one friend in Paris who would be just perfect for the job—if he could get hold of him. He couldn't. The switchboard operator at Police Judiciare headquarters on the Quai des Orfèvres told him Commissaire Claude Lebel never came into the office on Monday these days. No, they could not divulge his home number. Try again tomorrow morning. With that he had to be content, but with Sandra and Charlie for company, and Sheila Dohanyi's impeccable household staff to look after them, that presented no hardship for Rupert. They don't breed soft-shelled crabs in the Tyrol, but the *poulet* Sophia Loren was delicious.

Tuesday morning promptly at nine he phoned Paris again, and at five minutes past ten Claude Lebel phoned him.

"*Mon vieux,* how nice to hear your voice. What can I do for you?" For a semi-retired invalid, Claude sounded almost robust, and Rupert said so with obvious relish.

"Ah, my dear Rupert, it is springtime in Paris. Even I am not too old or too ill to make my feeble response."

The thought of that lugubrious, pain-racked old face, with its droopy moustache and cheeky eyes, savouring the joys of spring gave Rupert a piquant amusement. Lebel was nearly seventy and had officially been retired for several years now, but his experience as a detective and his unique reputation for discretion when dealing with highly sensitive and often byzantine political complexities were such that successive Ministers of the Interior refused to let him go. He held no official position anymore, and the rheumatic pains in his legs rendered him virtually immobile, but he dragged himself up from his little villa at Ivry three days a week to give whatever advice the head of Direction de la Surveillance du Territoire, DST, might feel in need of. He and Rupert had worked together off and on for years on art fraud cases and allied matters, and kept their friendship in good repair.

"I have a problem, Claude. If you have the time?"

"Time? My dear fellow. Time is the only thing I have plenty of. Health, no. Money, no. But time, plenty. Things are fairly quiet here at present—

since our Palestinian friends shifted their murder squads elsewhere. No knowing how long it will last. Tell me your problem."

Rupert gave him the essential facts relating to the Schellenberg Andrea di Guisto and its spurious provenance—the Duveen letter. One never wasted time giving Claude anything but the essential facts; his methodical brain spewed out nonessentials. The Duveen letter would be sent to him by special courier from Basle today, and he would start enquiries straight away, commencing with the cagey Monsieur Adelbert at Gaston Fonçier et Cie.

Rupert and Sandra spent the rest of the day working on the six paintings of what he now referred to as "the meat-truck collection." The "modern copy of something probably done in Rome about the turn of the century" yielded up its secret with little resistance: A scrawl in black paint across one corner on the back of the canvas which he deciphered as "School of Alfredo Pallantare circa 1800" was dismissed with one curt word, "Balls!"

It was a pretty little picture which might easily have fooled the uninitiated; peasants tending sheep amidst Romanesque ruins. Not at all Pallantare's *oeuvre*. The technique was that of a reasonably accomplished late nineteenth-century amateur who might well have had reason to be proud of his handiwork. But the outer edge of the canvas, which would normally have been hidden by a frame, clearly showed the name of a well-known manufacturer in Perugia who was certainly not in business in the fourteenth or eighteenth centuries. Just for fun, he asked Sandra to make a phone call to an assistant curator at the Uffizi in Florence who dealt with such matters. This yielded the information that the worthy canvas weaver, one Luigi Bastiani, had first set up shop in 1889.

The Gerini and the Aretino had both been listed in one of Berenson's essays on "Homeless Pictures" as early as 1932, and subsequently identified in a little church outside Verona. "Conveniently on the German Army's line of retreat in nineteen forty-five," Rupert commented. The Veronese authorities would probably have little trouble in staking a claim to them.

The one he had at first thought to attribute to Bartolomeo Cristiani began to give rise to doubts. There was no visible signature anywhere, which was not unusual, but the more he studied it the more familiar the scene became. It was of a singularly aristocratic saintly lady with two angels holding up a flowered curtain behind her for some arcane reason known only to the painter and themselves. There were two more kneeling on either side of her, and two at her feet, one playing a harp and the other a viol. Altogether an uncommon arrangement, and one that, once seen, lingered in a trained memory. At the moment, his memory was playing him tricks. He and Sandra ploughed once again through the voluminous collection of Berenson's invaluable photographs. It was nearly half an hour before Sandra said, "I think this may be it."

With magnifying glass and floodlights they painstakingly compared the photograph with the painting. It was perfect in every visible detail. The catch was that on the back of the photograph the master himself had written very clearly: "St. Lucy. In the gallery of Yale University, New Haven, Connecticut."

Rupert's memory did an abrupt switch back on track.

"Of course. St. Lucy. Rare bird, that one. I saw her when I lectured at a summer school at Yale. Nineteen sixty-three, I think it was. Berenson was a Harvard man to his fingertips. He wouldn't have given Yale such satisfaction unless he was absolutely certain. This one's a copy."

He went over the canvas again with the magnifying glass, and then said, "But it's a very fine copy. And unless I'm very wrong a very old one." He stood back and turned another thousand watt lamp on to the painting from an oblique angle.

"Something that always mystifies me," Sandra said. "How can you be sure?"

"Well, I can't, actually. If they really want to know, the quickest way would be to send it to Vienna for radio-carbon dating. That new unit they have at the Albertina would tell them to within fifty years or so. The canvas is surely medieval, for a start. But look at the paint cracks. They're quite characteristic of fourteenth-century north-Italian paints. The angle of the light throws them into relief. One can see much more depth this way. Fine, fine hairlines, quite irregular in pattern. Notice especially the blues. The Renaissance painters used lapis lazuli almost exclusively. I've no doubt spectometer testing will confirm this. After Prussian Blue was invented—which has a copper base—about seventeen hundred, one would expect to see quite a different structure of the cracks; more regular in pattern, the depth of two, maybe three, hairlines. Since it can't be Cristiani, it must have been painted before seventeen hundred, and nobody took much interest in copying these things in the intervening centuries. I'm going to say it's 'school of Cristiani, probably about fourteen hundred,' and for anyone interested in collecting fine paintings instead of famous names, it's worth ten thousand pounds of anyone's money. Might even buy it myself. It would look perfect in the Schellenberg collection."

It was nearly one o'clock when the Dohanyi's butler knocked on the farm office door. In view of the superb weather, the temperature on the terrace of the Schloss was just touching twenty degrees Celsius, he had taken the liberty of serving their lunch out there.

The terrace was exactly what Sheila had designed it to be, a perfect setting for a superbly cooked lunch of simple, unadorned country food, grilled trout taken from the local stream, fresh vegetables from the garden, a succulent Emmenthaler from a cheese factory not ten kilometres away, and all washed down with a clean, fresh-tasting white wine which had started life not many years ago along the banks of the Danube.

"Just one thing missing," Rupert murmured contentedly as he sipped his wine, watching the sunbeams through the tall glass.

"What's that?" Sandra asked.

"Your father would have had a gypsy orchestra playing for us."

"Yes, I suppose he would," she said wistfully. "Did you ever know my father?"

"Only as a small boy. We all spent a holiday at Semmering once. Before you were born, I'm afraid."

"Don't sound so dreadfully old," she said, gently mocking him. "This is bliss, of course. What a way to have a week's rest!"

Wondering how he had been permitted to get

through his lunch without Charlie's customary insistence on sharing it, he discovered the Welsh terrier's attention was preoccupied in the romantic
pursuit of Sheila's huge Labrador bitch. Poor Charlie!

The afternoon's work did not take long. The last
two paintings were a pair of beautiful altar panels
signed by Giovanni del Biondo, and Rupert's memory about them turned out to be correct. His notes
from the illicit visit to the farm-house at Frauenstein
in 1976 confirmed they were amongst the many
missing treasures he had been able to get a glimpse
of. In his old MFA files Sandra had found them
mentioned as having been looted from the palatial
Vienna home of the Schliemann family. Old Adolf
Schliemann, a prominent Jewish banker, had been
one of the consortium Baron Louis von Rothschild
had reluctantly put together at the insistence of
Chancellor Kurt Schnussnig to save the government's bankrupt Agricultural Bank in 1937. Like
the others, his family had soon suffered the full horror of Nazi spite and persecution. He had also been
a great admirer of the Siennese school of the *tre-
cento*, the thirteen hundreds, to which Biondo belonged. As Schliemann's collection had been exhibited publicly in 1935, a copy of the actual catalogue
was also in the file.

"Wonder what they will do with these," Rupert
mused. "Last time one of the Schliemann collection
turned up no member of the family could be found
to claim it. Must still be a dozen of their paintings in
the old monastery at Mauerbach. Pity to let these
two joined them in permanent darkness."

"I can remember mother talking about the Schliemanns," Sandra said. "Was the whole family wiped out by the Nazis?"

"So far as I know. If memory serves me, we once traced someone of that name we thought might be a cousin of some kind. Usual story; an ex-lawyer from Salzburg I think he was. Found him working as a labourer on a kibbutz in Galilee. Didn't want to know anything about it. You'll write up my report for Jo, won't you."

"Yes, darling man," Sandra said, with a sigh.

Tony and Sheila returned in time for dinner.

Wednesday morning was glorious in every way. The Alpine sun rolled through Rupert's bedroom window from the banks of the radiant mountain-sides enveloping him like a gentle avalanche. At ten o'clock he was still sipping coffee while digesting croissants and the delightful mysteries of Geoffrey Wills' lovely book on Chinese jade carvings, a subject in which he still regarded himself a rank amateur. But, naturally, it couldn't last. He was consumed in the fascinating exercise of trying to rationalize the remarkable belief of a Taoist philosopher of the fourth century A.D., a certain Ho Kung, that gold and jade "inserted into the nine apertures of a human corpse will preserve the body from putrefaction" when the phone rang. It was Lebel from Paris.

"News, *mon ami?*"

"I think we have found your man, Rupert."

"That's quick work."

"The world of fancy letter papers is a small one. Jean-Paul Lucas, one of my old protégés, had nothing important on his desk yesterday, so he did the leg work for me."

"Good. I am grateful, Claude. Did Monsieur Adelbert come up trumps then?"

"Not quite that easy. Adelbert couldn't trace it. He suggested Lucas try Dormier Frères, who said try Victor Hoche. They, in turn, passed him on to a little shop tucked in a wall just off the Place de l'Opéra. An old man there had known Leduc. He remembered the paper and that Leduc had gone out of business in nineteen fifty-seven. They spent most of the afternoon sifting through his old ledgers. Lucas tells me there weren't many buyers for this sort of stuff, and only one which would seem to fit your picture. In May nineteen fifty-three they sold a box of it to a regular customer, an art dealer called Leon Strassbourger, in the Boulevard des Capucines."

"That sounds like my man. Strassbourger? Don't know him myself, but Schellenberg bought from him at one time. Know anything about him?"

"Lucas remembered the name. Our computers don't go back that far, but our records do. Strassbourger served eight years in prison for collaboration with the Nazis during the Occupation. He was some kind of informer."

"Was he now? That might well tie up, mightn't it? Been in any trouble since then?"

"Nothing definite. I'm having a full dossier prepared on him. He's been suspected of dealing in works of art smuggled out of the Communist countries, but always kept on the right side of the law here, as far as we know. Paris is always full of rumours about these matters. They amuse the press, but we have no reason to investigate them unless someone lays a charge and requests us to. What do you want me to do now?"

"Just complete the dossier, if you will please,

Claude. Looks as though I'll have to come to Paris and see Monsieur Strassbourger myself. I may need your help."

"Gladly."

As he finished dressing half an hour later, it crossed Rupert's mind that it might be useful to know where Miss Schellenberg was at the moment. Just in case. He put a call through to the Connaught in London where an assistant manager informed him that she was visiting in Gloucestershire but was expected back some time on Friday. No, Miss Schellenberg had left no address or phone number. Miss Schellenberg never left an address or phone number. She had instructed them that she would be back on Friday. Rupert had no doubt at all she would be.

Chapter 10

Late the following Sunday afternoon, May 28, Rupert found himself, wearily but happily, gliding up the well of five flights of ancient stone stairs in a modern elevator in one of the places he loved best, the Ile St. Louis, in Paris. The Chambois lived in a spacious high-ceilinged apartment, sumptuously furnished à la Louis XIV at 16 Quai d'Anjou, while the Dohanyis kept a small modern *pied-à-terre* one floor above. When Sheila Dohanyi heard that Rupert had to go to Paris for a few days, she said, "But of course, please use our flat. Madame Mercier complains that we never go there." Madame Mercier, a housewife from the Auvergne, was the widow of a yeoman farmer, and her vocation was keeping house for the Chambois, and the Dohanyis on their rare visits. Since Cameron and Louise were away in Canada at a conference concerning aviation legal complications, Rupert knew he would have the attentions of the inestimable Madame Mercier all to himself.

The last three days at Schönberg had been rest-
ful, both physically and mentally. The weather continued blissful and the Dohanyis busy, leaving Rupert and Sandra to their own devices, except at
dinner *à la quatre,* which were always lively and delightful. While Charlie pursued his unrequited romance with Sheila's Labrador bitch, they read,
walked in the gardens and across the fields and hill-
sides, and talked—mostly talked. About art, business, Austria, music; about almost anything except
themselves. Although it was nearly three years since
Sandra had fled the wreckage of her brief, disastrous marriage in New York, this was the first time
they had ever had three totally uninterrupted days
together.

Both were grateful for the opportunity, but when
a man and a woman are so closely involved in each
other's lives a veil of reticence sometimes grows up
between them, springing principally from an overwhelming desire never to hurt, or risk being hurt.
When they have become indispensable to each
other, are first cousins, and the man old enough to
be the woman's father, the veil can become impene-
trable. The thought of marriage was always there
but never mentioned.

Rupert had lived alone for twenty-five years. He
knew himself to be a compassionate man, but he
had grown accustomed to having his own way,
about nearly everything. In particular he liked his
own way of comfort and relaxation; he had developed it to the point of being a fine art. Suppose
there were children? He could not convince himself
that he was prepared to undertake the burdens of
fatherhood at this stage of his life.

He had thought of Sandra in the role of mistress;

of course he had. Every time he kissed her good-night and she climbed the stairs to her own apartment, and every time he saw her in those low-cut clinging evening dresses which so became her, he couldn't help thinking about it. But such a relationship carried its own unwelcome risks and responsibilities. In this so called "permissive age" he clung even harder than ever to his moral integrity. He could face any church service as a penitent, not as a practising hypocrite, and he believed, with some degree of assurance, that Sandra felt the same. He was sure this was the reason she practically never asked him to come up to her apartment. What could such a relationship do to a sensitive, cultured woman like her? Had he the right to gamble? Just to see what might happen? God knows, there were times when he found the temptation well nigh overwhelming. He was no monk. There had been other women in his life after Alexie had died. But never one who affected him the way this one did.

If he had had the gift of mind reading he might have discovered that Sandra's was a mirror of his own. Their brief idyll was joyous, but neither got any closer to solving the riddle.

Madame Mercier, who visited friends in the country every Sunday, had left a note saying that a cold supper and a bottle of chablis awaited him in the refrigerator. There was also a telegram addressed to him on the hall table. It came from London and told him that Miss Schellenberg could come over to Paris for a day if it was really important, but it would have to be before Thursday when she had to return to Chicago. Not much time. A third letter was from the Quai des Orfèvres telling him that, although *le Patron* never came up to the office on a Monday, Jean-Paul Lucas would be there tomorrow morning and would be happy to go over the Strassbourger dossier if Rupert cared to come round to see him. Lucas added that *le Patron* had told him Monsieur Conway would expect the entire resources of the Department of the Interior to be placed at his disposal, and while he could not promise quite so much, he would gladly do his best to be helpful.

Rupert mused over these sheets of paper in good humour for a moment and then put them back on the table. He turned to the big northward-facing window and stood gazing out at the romance of Paris on a fine spring evening. He could see all the way to Sacré-Coeur perched atop Montmartre, its west side glowing pink in the fading sunlight, its east pale blue in the shadow. That was a sight to embrace all clichés. What could there possibly be about it of the remotest value that had not already been said? What idiot would have the conceit to think he could improve on Dumas and Hugo?

Rupert went to the kitchen to fetch the promised chablis and chicken in aspic, put it on a silver tray and settled himself before the big window in the deepest armchair he could find. Then, with an audible sigh of content, he took a book from his attaché case. His mind rapidly floated back across the Alps and out into the Adriatic with Jack Higgins. Funnily enough, he knew well the wild marshes of Albania that master of adventure was writing about.

Only on the previous Friday morning had a much strengthened but wildly impatient and fully bearded Guiseppe Giancollo, née Horst Rheinberg, been released from St. Vincent de Paul. He dived straight into the Metro and took the first train to the Place de l'Opéra. As he was coming up the steps into the Place de l'Opéra he happened to spot Louis in the throng ascending just ahead of him. His first thought was to catch up with him and enter into genial conversation, but some instinctive caution bred into him during years of police service caused him to have second thoughts. Instead, he hung back, kept within the crowd, and studied his quarry from a safe distance.

Instead of crossing over the Boulevard des Capucines, to Horst's surprise Louis walked straight down the north side. Horst dropped behind as close as he dared. They crossed the Rue Edouard VII and just opposite Strassbourger's store Louis suddenly dropped into a chair at a curb-side table of a café. Horst stopped abruptly in the entrance of the Wagons-Lits travel bureau and pretended to study the railway timetables. He was covered from the street, but the back of Louis' head was clearly visible. Louis took out a copy of *Figaro* and appeared to be reading it. He dropped a couple of sheets of the paper onto the pavement, and a moment later a waiter came out to take his order. It wasn't long in coming. Louis sipped his coffee somewhat nervously and, turning the pages of his newspaper, upset the mineral water all over the table. Then another man, appearing from the direction of the Madeleine, sat down at the same table. Louis took a paper napkin and started to wipe the mineral water off the table. He seemed to be apologizing to the newcomer for the mess he had made. They got into conversation, apparently casually, and as the man looked at Louis, Horst was staring straight at him.

He recognized him at once. They had worked on

the same floor in the Frankfurteralle for two years during his last posting before going to Leipzig. The man's name was Gebler, and his business was Intelligence. Horst's mind started racing, and for a few seconds a kind of panic overcame him. He shuffled his feet, almost stumbled backwards, and nearly knocked down a portly and irate woman coming out of the Wagons-Lits. She gasped out a throaty *"Nom de Dieu!"* and gave him a withering look; he mumbled some attempt at apology.

Horst half-turned so he could survey both sides of the street without exposing himself too much. The first question to be answered: Was Gebler alone? His experienced eyes looked warily round searching for any sign of the classic shadowing formation. Two this side, three across the street and a scout who floats out ahead of you. Nothing. He came out a little into the open, deliberately exposing a target. No one suddenly ducked into a doorway. No one was looking at him. Gebler and Louis were deep in conversation, and neither of them knew him well enough to spot him at this distance, wearing a beard.

Start with the facts, they always taught you. Speculation and deduction come later. The big question, "Is Gebler here looking for me?" was unanswerable at the moment. Quite possibly he was. There could be limitless other possibilities as well. The newspaper and the upset glass were dead giveaways. Standard recognition technique in the trade. Why was he talking to Louis? The unwelcome answer to that one was almost certainly the only one. Louis must be an SSD informer; the one referred to in the files simply as "our source." That fitted; he looked the type. In which case, Gebler just might be paying one of his usual routine visits, making the periodic assessment of reliability of "sources." It was part of the drill. Might be. There was no reason to think the "source" would have any information concerning Guiseppe Giancollo. Strassbourger had not asked for a name and he had not volunteered one. But it would be the kind of information that would interest Gebler. Horst turned eastward again and walked slowly back to the Metro, descended the steps into the ticket hall and entered a phone booth.

For at least another few minutes he could be sure Strassbourger would not be encumbered by his shadow. The dealer seemed relieved, even glad to hear from him. No, he did not yet have a buyer, but he was now satisfied that the paintings were saleable, and at a good price. Amongst other things, that conveyed that nobody was looking for them, which was reassuring. Strassbourger gave every indication of seeming genuinely anxious to do business. Several times he used Italian words, which seemed some indication he had no doubts about Horst's assumed nationality. He expressed no surprise at the signor's insistence that next time Strassbourger must come to him. That was not unusual in his trade, but a meeting was not possible before Monday at lunchtime. Horst didn't argue.

They agreed to meet at a little café just behind the Hôtel de Ville at noon. Horst would not bring the paintings, but they would be close by if a deal was in sight. The dealer fully understood the signor's emphasis on complete confidentiality; that was how he preferred all his transactions to be done. In the art world, discretion was customary. Horst went back to his hotel just off the Quai de Bercy, reorganized his luggage once again, checked most of it

135

into a locked luggage compartment at the Gare de Lyon, and went off to Fontainebleau for the weekend.

At just about the same time Anna, her usually inexhaustible *savoir faire* at last beginning to search out a possible point of exhaustion brought on by sixteen straight hours in the unwelcome company of the irritating Klaus Bach, was pacing up and down the concrete outside the circular entrances of Charles de Gaulle Airport. There was no sign of the car and chauffeur she had been assured would be on hand to meet them. It would have been easy to get into a taxi. It would have been easy for the embassy to send one of their innumerable fleet. No. Out of the question. The usual mania of Russian bureaucracy for turning the simplest exercise into a byzantine conspiracy had made it imperative that she be met by some kind of undercover agent dressed like a Seine river pilot and driving a blue Italian car with a Normandy licence plate. Nothing remotely resembling such a vehicle having put in an appearance after twenty minutes, Anna's practical Gallic streak asserted itself, and to Bach's horror she stepped into the first available taxi and ordered him to do likewise. She had no hesitation in instructing the driver to take them to a run-down, rambling old office building that was the Paris headquarters of the KGB; appropriately enough, just round the corner from the Place de la Bastille. The Head of Station was her last boss under whom she had served before being promoted to equivalent rank when he was sent to Paris. Anna knew perfectly well he knew she knew as well as he did that the DST knew exactly where his office was, and she was in no mood for any more silly games.

They paid off the taxi driver and entered the grubby, litter-strewn lobby. Its dirty, bare plaster walls were decorated only with the usual clutter of sign boards and tattered posters: urging the unsuspecting passer-by to attend a "Workers' Rally" at the Velodrome five Sundays ago to protest the Vietnamese invasion of Cambodia; to attend at your nearest hospital to give blood to the French Red Cross; to remind property owners that their Municipale taxes were due on the first of last April and delinquents were subject to dire penalties; and to warn that anyone found peddling pornographic literature on the premises would be fined and have his wares confiscated! Such practical people, the French.

Next to a large scrawl proclaiming one of the two decrepit-looking elevators "Out of Order" was a list of the building's occupants. Messieurs Ganne et Veber, customs brokers; L. G. St. Gervais et Fils didn't say what they did; Maison de Pantin, importers of Oriental novelties; etc. The whole of the third floor appeared to be given over to the activities of the Agence Maritime de la Mer Noire. That was as good a cover as any. They got into the one working elevator and pressed the button marked 3. It went straight past 3 and landed them at 4. Anna was too old a hand at this game to waste time pressing number 3 again. They found the door leading to the staircase and walked down one flight. Bach stumbled with the luggage and Anna retrieved her own satchel, swinging it over her shoulder. Inevitably, the solid hard-wood door on the third floor was locked. She wrote out the name of the Head of Station on a sliver of paper, put a five digit number beside it, and slid it under the door leaving a half inch clearly visible on the outside. Then she ordered Bach to start banging on the door and not stop until the paper disappeared. In about two minutes it did. They waited another three minutes in silence and then there were sounds of unbolting and unlocking. In due course the heavy door was opened and an old man in blue overalls peered cautiously out. Two burly men with their hands ominously thrust into their coat pockets were visible behind him. Anna said some Russian words, and they gestured to the old one to admit her and her companion. Without ceremony Anna and Bach followed them down a long corridor. The contrast with the rest of the building was striking—walls and floor were immaculately clean and well kept, the lighting was brilliant. The old man disappeared and one of the goons unlocked a second door which led into an office that might very well have housed an "Agence Maritime." Men and women sat at neatly arranged desks, studying papers, pounding typewriters, talking into telephones. They stopped outside another door marked "Monsieur le Directeur" and the goon knocked deferentially. A tall, swarthy man with a clipped military moustache opened it. Anna and Bach were ushered into the sanctum sanctorum, just as Gebler and his Russian overseer entered the building to make their report.

Chapter 11

Over most of northwest Europe nature continued
her stunning performance for another week-end.
The parks, lakes and rivers happily seethed with relaxing humanity; the city pavements were deserted
everywhere more than a few metres from the nearest
sidewalk café and the main routes leading out of
town. Signor Giancollo enjoyed the quiet anonymity
of a simple *auberge* in the woods near Fontainebleau, slept better than he had since leaving Leipzig
two weeks earlier and gazed with wonderment at the
fantastic luxury of the ordinary French working
people's Sunday lunches.

Only for members of the East German SSD and
some of their immediate Russian taskmasters was it
a week-end of frustrated boredom and discomfort.
Boris Valishnikov was still stuck in the cramped,
uncomfortable office of the Consulate in Milan,
trying to find his way through the gloomy and psy-
chopathic underworld of the Red Brigades. All day
Friday Klaus Bach and his hastily summoned legion

had haunted the Boulevard des Capucines without any result. Time and again Louis had raised the matter of the anonymous Italian with his employer; the only response he received was a noncommittal shrug and comment to the effect that "it was to be expected"; such behaviour was common enough on the twilight fringe of the art business. Perhaps the man would come back next week. Or the week after. The practise of telling one's assistants as little as possible was also very common. From Friday night until Monday morning Bach's men had spent long, tedious and fruitless hours in a large old-fashioned apartment block near the Porte d'Orleans running up and down stairs, drifting in and out of countless cafés and bars, buying unwanted cigarettes and newspapers at kiosks, all in the process of watching Leon Strassbourger in the hope of finding Horst Rheinberg. The art dealer was their only lead to the elusive Italian picture seller the "source" had so carefully described to Gebler; a description that might, or might not, fit that of the much-sought-after SSD defector. All they got for their trouble were endlessly dull views of the traffic hurtling along the Route Peripherique and many doleful ones of Montrouge Cemetery. It didn't make them happy. They would have been unhappier still had they known that amongst the crowds who drifted in and out of the sidewalk cafés all day in the neighbourhood of the Place du 25 Août 1944 there were never less than three DST men watching them.

In the Frankfurteralle, Abrassimov's office and KGB headquarters in Moscow, they were beginning to get a little hysterical about the whole operation. Nearly two weeks had now gone by since Rheinberg's disappearance. Major alerts in both London and Washington had been unable to detect any of the ripples which usually accompany the arrival of an important defector. Comrade Brehznev had retired once again to his dacha at Odintsovo with another attack of his blood pressure trouble. Days of frantic activity at Frauenstein had failed to unearth anything resembling a detailed inventory of what was there in the dozens of long-sealed and dusty packing crates. They had arrested the aged caretaker and were holding him in solitary confinement for questioning, just in case anyone could think of a new question to ask him.

Her rare visits to Paris always raised Anna's spirits. She could spend her free time wandering the streets wondering whether her mother had been there forty or fifty years before. She was senior enough and sufficiently trusted to be allowed the privilege of a little privacy. She had earned it. The relief from the constant presence of Bach, with his ceaseless trumpet voluntaries of self-justification, was a joy in itself. There was a top-priority job to be done, she was still head office's senior representative on the spot, and the KGB never gives up; but until the local KGB and Bach's men picked up the trail of Rheinberg again there was nothing she could do. On Saturday night she went to the Comedie Française with her ex-boss and his wife, and on Sunday afternoon she took a boat trip down the Seine as far as Ivry where she chanced to meet an old friend. It was all a refreshing change from the pressure and tension of her usual work.

At a quarter to nine on Monday morning Leon Strassbourger kissed his ill and aging wife good-bye, and walked around the corner to the Porte d'Orleans Metro station where he caught the train to work as usual. Quite unbeknownst to him he was escorted by a contingent of SSD operatives who, unbeknownst to them, were, in turn, being followed by DST men who had all the advantages of playing on their own home ground. Strassbourger reached his office without incident and all concerned prepared themselves to put in another dull and uneventful day's work of watching.

At a quarter to ten Rupert sauntered the length of the Ile St. Louis, over the bridge that joins it to the Ile de la Cité, around Notre Dame and arrived in Jean-Paul Lucas' office on the Quai des Orfèvres at two minutes to the hour. They had not met before, but their mutual regard for Claude Lebel formed an instant bond of trust and confidence. That, and the fact that Lucas was yet another of the dedicated band of pipe lovers. No, he had never met Jo Liebmann. The dossier the Department had compiled on the art dealer Leon Strassbourger was produced, and they went through it with meticulous care. Strassbourger had been born in Molsheim, a small town in Alsace-Lorraine, in 1915, and had spent most of his childhood there. Under the Treaty of Versailles the area, annexed by Germany after the War of 1870, had been restored to France in 1919, and some time thereafter his father, Pierre Strassbourger, had gone to Paris where he prospered and in due course became proprietor of a thriving art business in the Boulevard des Capucines. The family appeared to have been somewhat divided as there was no record of Leon's mother ever having come to live in Paris. It seems she had died in Metz

142

in 1937 when the boy left the polytechnic and came to join his father in the business.

In 1939 Leon had been exempted from military service on health grounds and having grade E-minus eyesight. He lived with his father in an apartment over the store, where he worked throughout the whole of the Occupation. The father died in 1943. There was no record of anything untowards throughout the years 1940 to 1945, but shortly after the end of World War II interrogation of returning French prisoners-of-war led to the discovery that Leon had been involved in some kind of informers' network, collaborating with the Nazis. He was arrested and, although the evidence was flimsy, had refused legal counsel and put up little defence. He had been found guilty and sentenced to twelve years imprisonment, which because of his good behaviour and precarious health was later commuted to eight. He came out of prison in 1953, obtained the lease of his father's old premises and rapidly reestablished himself in the business. He married an Alsatian woman in 1955, and had lived ever since in a large block at 109 Avenue Ernest Reyner near the Porte d'Orleans. So far as was known he had never taken part in political activities of any kind or had any interests outside his business and his home. His name had several times been linked to rumours of dealing in paintings of dubious ownership, but no complaint had ever been filed against him. That was all.

Jean-Paul returned the Duveen letter to Rupert confirming what he already knew, that even if the signature was proved a forgery, the fact that Duveen had been dead since 1939 made it little more than a minor criminal curiosity. It might well be used as pressure to make Strassbourger talk, but there would be little point in trying to press any charge against him. Rupert decided to go and poke round the shop in the Boulevard des Capucines and invited Lucas to have dinner with him that evening at the Quasimodo, an invitation the Deputé Commissaire gladly accepted.

Rupert decided he wished to be a bit more mobile so he went to the Avis office in the Rue de Ponthieu and hired a pint-sized bright red Renault. After driving three times round the Place de l'Opéra he found a parking space and walked leisurely to Leon Strassbourger's store. It pleasantly surprised him. It wasn't Stephensplatz, and it certainly wasn't Walker's Gallery, but it was large and airy. The paintings in the window were of average to good quality, though he personally never liked mixing modern and old canvases in the same display. The place had all the appearances of a respectable, well-run establishment. Glancing at his watch he noticed it was nearly eleven-fifteen, and without having any very clear idea of what he was about to do, beyond adopting the role of a casual American visitor, he walked inside. His luck was in; there were five people in the store going about what appeared to be their lawful business, and one of them was a frail-looking little man of at least sixty-odd years wearing thick gold-rimmed glasses.

A smartly dressed young woman came forward and asked if she could be of any assistance. Rupert replied, not just at present, and hoped they wouldn't mind if he browsed round a bit. The front of the store was mainly taken up with modern French paintings of a genre he understood, mostly rivers and bridges and farm-houses and hills covered with vines; fairly hackneyed subjects, but by and large the artists showed both talent and craftsmanship—a rare quality these days, alas. He noticed the prices ranged from about a thousand francs up to nearly twenty, and at present levels he reckoned it was about right. There were some quite lovely heads of small children by a Spanish artist he had never heard of before and he made a note of the name. And the prices.

Farther back the walls were heavily lined with older works at much higher prices. Seventeenth-century French painters, some quite nice Dutch stuff, and mixed in with them all there were even a few Italians. To his delight he discovered an unidentified saint who claimed to have been painted by Nicolo di Pietro Gerini. He had to resist the impulse to pull out his jeweller's eye-glass. It would have put the "casual tourist" pose in jeopardy, but he decided there was a good chance the claim might well be justified. It ought to be at the price—eighty thousand francs. It would have made a nice mate for the Gerini in the meat-truck collection back in Innsbruck. Rupert decided to ad-lib it from there. His evident interest in the top end of the store's price range had little difficulty in catching the owner's attention. Rupert, wanting to make everything as easy as possible for him, opened the batting.

"Lovely painting this."

"Indeed, monsieur. You know Gerini's work?"

That little touch of professionalism appealed to Rupert right away. Always start by subtly flattering the potential customer. He must be careful not to give away that he played both sides of the street himself.

"No, not really. But I have a friend back home who has one. I've often admired it."

"I think your friend would be jealous if you had this one in your collection, monsieur."

Despite Strassbourger's ghastly war record, and his rather unprepossessing appearance, he found it difficult not to like a man who understood his craft as well as this. He thought it best to duck.

"Thanks very much. You flatter me. This is way out of my league." He deliberately used the word *ligneur*, the wrong word. It was always a rule of his when opening conversation with someone in a language not his own, to let them get the impression his mastery of it was less than perfect. The object in this game was to occupy strategic ground, not make a grand impression. That might, or might not, be useful later.

Strassbourger's smiling response was again absolutely correct.

"There are many painters of a similar style and period whose work does not command such high prices as Gerini, monsieur."

Rupert had no way of knowing that the little dealer had one especially in mind at that very moment. His own problem was one of balance. If he was going to get any useful information out of Strassbourger, it was essential to get him onto Duveen's ground without losing his own strategic advantage. There was no way he could force the man to tell him what he wanted to know.

All he said was, "Yes, I suppose there are."

That really wasn't good enough. He mentally kicked himself for not being cleverer. They chatted inconsequentially for a few minutes, when Rupert noticed his adversary making frequent glances at his watch. He had suddenly acquired the air of a man whose mind was somewhere else. If Rupert didn't get the discussion back into charted waters quickly this fish showed signs of swimming right off his line altogether.

"What could you show me at about, say, half the price of the Gerini?" he hazarded.

It wasn't a very good shot but by happy chance that was exactly the price range of which Strassbourger had been thinking.

"I have nothing here at the moment," came the reply, "but I am in touch with a client who has something that might interest monsieur. Actually, I am seeing him later today."

He looked at his watch again in a manner that conveyed the thought "and not very much later."

"Hmm. That might be interesting." He had a vision of Miss Schellenberg getting on that plane to Chicago Thursday morning. He really only had until tomorrow night to be sure of landing her.

"Yes, I think that would interest me. How long would it take?" he asked, trying to walk a fine line consistent both with holding the dealer's interest and not prejudicing the tourist act.

"Only a day or two," came the response.

"Hmm," he hesitated again. "I have to leave Paris tomorrow night."

For the first time he noticed a young man with a face exactly like a weasel hovering in the background, and Strassbourger's reply came several decibels lower.

"Perhaps if monsieur would care to come back about six o'clock this evening . . . I could keep the store open to receive him," he practically whispered.

He was happy to work late for the chance of a forty-thousand-franc sale, and he never liked the staff hanging around when he was dealing with "difficult" paintings.

Monsieur responded in equally conspiratorial tones that he would care to very much. Strassbourger made a little bow and promptly retired, leaving the hovering young man staring blankly into space.

As Rupert walked back to his parking place behind the Opéra he heard the bells of a nearby church ring out twelve o'clock, reminding him he had just five minutes to move the Renault before it would most certainly receive the attentions of the ever-alert Traffic Police. He also noticed that the sky was beginning to cloud over. Deciding to enjoy the fine weather before the now threatening break brought it to an abrupt end, he drove the car back to the Quai d'Anjou, hurriedly ate the snack lunch Madame Mercier insisted on preparing for him, and wandered across to the little park at the east end of the island where the benches and the gravel paths were covered with a delicate blue mantle provided by the falling petals of the jacaranda trees. Some time not too long after six o'clock this evening he had to make his attempt at confronting Strassbourger with the Duveen letter and, much more difficult, somehow continue to keep him in a cooperative frame of mind—even if he had to bribe him by buying a forty-thousand-franc painting he didn't want. The price didn't worry him too much. If Strassbourger could sell it for that price, he had little doubt of his own ability to do so. There was no better way of occupying the afternoon than by considering all the angles and trying to work out a plausible plan of attack. As he gazed across the Seine at the optimistic spectacle of some small boys trying to catch an edible fish in those murky waters the first thought that struck him was, just what impulse had driven him to this self-imposed and improbable adventure? Professional curiosity entered into it, of course—anything connected with Lord Duveen had an attraction of its own—but the Andrea di Guisto was of no importance, and it was not as though he didn't have enough to do. As he thought of Andrea's humble altarpiece it took his mind back to his only visit to the convent of San Leonardo di Monte. Yes, that was where the germ had first taken hold. He hadn't thought about it for years, but the horror of what the British troops had found there was ineradicable in the memory of every man who saw it. The Wehrmacht had evacuated the area in good order and discipline two days before, and he had been travelling with the Corps reconnaissance troops seeking the retreating enemy.

He would never forget the stark hellishness of the sight that greeted him as his driver drove the jeep into the convent courtyard. The lovely old medieval buildings had been ransacked from end to end. Female clothing and furniture littered the yard, straggled from every shattered window; books and altar cloths and vestments lay half-burned in a heap next to a smashed gilt statue of the Virgin covered with human excrement and broken bottles. Puddles of blood and human flesh were everywhere. The few old nuns who were left alive they found hiding, terror stricken in a cellar. The pathetic graves they had managed to dig during the night for their younger sisters who had been raped, ravaged, mutilated and slaughtered to sate the bestial lust of a gang of dehumanized thugs were themselves enough to bring tears to the eyes of the toughest battle-scarred veteran. His driver, Corporal Bill Ford, a tough Australian who had driven all through the desert campaigns and from the beaches of Sicily right up to Florence under fire, had retched and then vomited violently.

There was only one corpse still to be seen; that of a man lying face downwards, his shoulder smashed open and his head half severed at the neck. The flies were swarming in the blood clotted all over his back and a blood-stained axe lay a few paces away. An axe swung by someone unknown, someone probably now dead, probably a woman, who was either fear-crazed or quite incredibly brave, and probably both. Of course, the corpse's uniform was the silver-trimmed black of an officer in the SS.

Rupert had to shake himself out of this ghoulish reverie; it still very nearly made him sick to remember it. He wondered what he would have to tell Lucas when they met for dinner. The first spot of rain began to fall and he heard a clap of thunder coming from somewhere the other side of Clichy. He sauntered back to the apartment to wait out the time until six o'clock.

Chapter 12

Leon Strassbourger emerged from a taxi a little hesitantly, a little painfully, as he did everything, and entered the Café du Hôtel de Ville at twenty-five minutes past twelve. He had not seen his nameless Italian "client" for ten days and had difficulty in spotting him behind the beard and the eccentric haircut. He had no regrets at being late, it was often good tactics for an assignation like this to make the clients wait a little; it often gave some indication of how hungry they were. But he was keen to do business. The client was clearly Italian, the paintings were Italian, and all of a good period. They were in excellent condition, and his extensive research had unearthed no trace of them in recent sales, nothing about church robberies anywhere in Italy remotely fitted them. By every measurement he could apply they were "clean" and undoubtedly of high quality. With more to come, the man had said. He stood just inside the doorway for nearly a minute mulling these things over in his mind, while his weak eyes strained round the crowded room searching for a familiar face. He felt the first fear of disappointment that the man might not have turned up. He was, fortunately or unfortunately, totally unaware of the trouble his sudden dash for a passing taxi had caused Gebler and the SSD team following him, and of the amusement this had created for the DST men who were following them.

Horst had arrived promptly at twelve as arranged and taken a table for two as far from the front door as possible, seating himself at an angle where he could see all who came in without presenting himself full face. He did not mind waiting, he had had plenty of experience in his police career. He saw Strassbourger the moment he entered but made no move. He let a full minute go by while the little man stood there craning his thin neck and beak-like nose in every direction, until he was satisfied that his new appearance served at least as a faint screen against easy recognition. It was only then that he made an effort to attract Strassbourger's attention.

They shook hands, two glasses of St. Raphael and Vichy water were ordered and they started to talk. Horst preferred to stick to Italian and his guest made no objection. He commented on his host's changed appearance quite naturally, was glad to see the bandage had gone from his forehead, thought the beard suited the signor very well. Horst accepted it in good grace, gave nothing away, nor did Strassbourger attempt any identification. With one eye firmly on the door Horst intently scrutinized every face that came through it. After only two sips of his drink he saw what he had feared. Two men came in almost shoulder to shoulder. One of them was Gebler; the other one looked familiar, but the name eluded him. Fortunately, the only table left available was right up front on the far side. Facts, Horst thought to himself. What are the facts? Number one, that the SSD still have an informer in Strassbourger's shop and that he works under Gebler. No surprises there. Number two, they are following Strassbourger as well. Question. Does he know? Can't be certain at this stage, but it seems unlikely from his relaxed behaviour; in their two meetings and one phone call Strassbourger had shown none of the symptoms of the sort of anxiety one would expect from a man who was far from robust and obviously of a nervous temperament. Next question. Why are they following him? Are they looking for me? A definite possibility. The only way to find out is to put it to the test and see what happens. An unwelcome complication at this particular moment, but it had to be done. There was more than curiosity at stake. It might be a matter of life or death. For him? Or Strassbourger? He was well able to take care of himself, but he wouldn't have given much for the frail little art dealer's chances against his old SSD colleagues. The Russians may have had a tough time trying to make good spies out of them, but killing came easy. And it was very much in his interests that the sickly little man be kept alive, at least for another twenty-four hours.

The waiter came for their order; both took the soup du jour, Strassbourger asked for *cotelettes d'agneau*, and after careful consideration Horst ordered a cheese soufflé; not because he intended to eat it, but because he knew that in any self-respecting French restaurant it would take at least forty minutes to prepare. He carefully noted the prices of everything. Another skill all good policemen have to learn is how to see out of the corners of their eyes; without ever looking directly at them one vital fraction of Horst's keen vision never left Gebler and his companion. Gebler had been forced to accept a seat with his back to him; the other man was sitting with his back to the wall and facing the table where Horst and Strassbourger were sitting at a forty-five degree angle. The man kept glancing their way but betrayed no visible reactions beyond obvious curiosity. Third question. Could they have known that Strassbourger was coming to see him? Since it was highly unlikely that they would be able to arrange a phone-tap on Strassbourger's store, which was almost entirely surrounded by banks and the Ministry of Justice, all of which were heavily guarded, the answer to that question was almost certainly not. Whatever came next was speculation, but the time taken to prepare the soufflé should give him ample opportunity to negotiate the sale of at least one painting and formulate a plan to test their shadows' intentions. He noted that it was not until after their soup had arrived that Gebler signalled a waiter to order lunch.

Whatever their intentions might be, it seemed reasonably certain they would not attempt any rough stuff in this crowded place, and as long as everyone remained where he was they were too far away to attempt any stiletto or needle tricks. Remembering some of the things their ingenious boys had been working on just before he quit the service, he was happy to notice neither of the shadows carried umbrellas. Before getting to the serious part of their meeting Horst decided to make one check. With a brief word of explanation to Strassbourger he got up and walked quickly to a nearby hallway marked "Toilets." A couple of metres down the hallway was a small open lobby inhabited by an ancient crone in a white overall whose sole item of occupational equipment was a large white plate upon which the clientele were expected to deposit coins in appreciation for what the French amusingly call "*le service*." The lady presided over an arrangement common throughout Europe in public places which do not cater to the tourist trade; behind her there was a thin fence-like partition between a little swing gate marked "*Hommes*" and another marked "*Femmes*," which gave each a small measure of privacy, but not much. Horst ducked quickly inside the one marked "*Femmes*," and was lucky enough to avoid both the crone's attention and to find it empty. Sure enough, a moment later he heard hurried footsteps approaching and heard the gate marked "*Hommes*" swing squeaking on its hinges. He was just quick enough to be able to identify Gebler's distinctive back view disappearing into "*Hommes*." He dropped a five-franc coin into the white plate, and within seconds was back in his seat. A moment later he had the innocent amusement of watching Gebler return to his table with a puzzled, worried look on his face. Strassbourger showed no sign of interest, or even awareness of the incident.

What had happened was no indication that Gebler knew who he was, but ample evidence he wanted to find out. Horst took another sip of his drink and quietly invited his guest to come straight to business. The dealer was fully cooperative. He was prepared to buy the three paintings he had examined for a hundred thousand francs. Horst did some quick sums. That was approximately fifty thousand deutschmarks: say, twenty-five thousand

U.S. dollars, or nearly thirteen thousand English pounds. It was probably half what they would fetch at a reputable auction, but he was in no position to attempt such a deal. It wasn't enough to buy a vineyard in the Argentine or anywhere else, but it would get him there comfortably, with money to spare, and nine other good canvases in hand. His master plan was still intact, more or less. The presence of Gebler and company had already convinced him that he would have to chance the local market in South America. It would be most unwise to hang about Paris one minute longer than it took to acquire sufficient money to finance the journey. It was probably the best deal he was likely to get.

He accepted, asking that the exchange be made hand-to-hand, and in the form of a certified banker's cheque payable at the Banque Française et Italianne in Paris. Strassbourger acknowledged that was not unusual in the trade; it could be easily arranged. The problem of effecting the exchange of the paintings was rather more complicated. And dangerous. Horst said he would like it to be done later that afternoon or early evening, at some place of his choosing, and that he would phone Strassbourger to finalize arrangements as soon as he could.

The long awaited soufflé arrived. Horst toyed with it while Strassbourger cut into his lamb chops. Another waiter arrived at Gebler's table with a tray and served their meal. The two SSD men tucked napkins under their chins and prepared to eat. The moment they cut into whatever it was in front of them Horst put a hundred-franc note under the edge of his plate, said softly, "Will phone you as soon after three as I can," and walked briskly to the door. Strassbourger looked surprised but said nothing.

Clients selling undocumented paintings frequently behaved like that, and this one was certainly a pretty cool, unemotional individual; especially for an Italian. He had noticed the client left the money for their lunch, which was at least evidence of good faith.

Just before Horst reached the door he noted grimly that his action had caused consternation at Gebler's table. He was quite experienced enough to know that there would be others waiting around outside, but one or both of these would have to make a hurried exit. He came out of the little restaurant and walked quickly to the Rue de Rivoli where he turned left. The street was crowded and the traffic heavy, as was to be expected at that time of day. There was neither time nor advantage in trying to count heads at this moment, but as he turned into the Rue de Rivoli he had a good view of Gebler frantically dodging traffic to cross the busy street and make for two men lounging against one of the rear doors of the Hôtel de Ville. He just had time to register that one of them wore a dark green suit and the other brown when he passed the corner of the massive building. He broke into a run and headed for the Metro. Just as he hit the turning to descend the steps brown suit and green suit appeared rounding the corner also at a run. Whether anybody else was forming a pack he couldn't tell. Whether they knew who he was or not was now just a matter of academic interest. At the very least they wanted a quiet little chat, and Horst had no wish to chat.

He went down the steps pressing against a hurrying and indifferent crowd coming up, and headed for the first exit on his left. He moved in close to the nearside wall and paused on the second step to look back. Whether green suit saw him or not he couldn't be sure. There was no sign of brown suit. He turned and sprinted up the steps. As soon as he reached street level again he paused to have a quick look round and saw brown suit standing at the top of the Rue de Rivoli steps in agitated discussion with two more men. He didn't waste time to see whether they spotted him or not but hurried straight into the entrance of the nearest department store. He saw the up-escalator just behind the ladies' lingerie counter and went up five floors as fast as he could without jostling the other passengers sufficiently to be remembered. At the top he found himself in the toy department where he was confronted by a horde of noisy children and an irate, harassed pair of school-teachers vainly trying to keep order. The "exit" sign was immediately behind this melée. He picked his way carefully through it and found himself on a service staircase where two men were struggling with a large packing case, ran down two flights to the third floor and went right across the store until he found a down-escalator which terminated at the back near an exit leading to the Rue St. Martin. There wasn't a taxi in sight so he walked straight across the street into a large ladies' clothing store and repeated the same manoeuvre. This time he came out into the Rue de Rivoli two blocks down from Place Hôtel de Ville and ran for a bus which was just starting up heading westward. He seated himself conveniently and watched the street behind with the closest attention.

The bus drove past the Louvre, Palais-Royale and along the wall of the Tuilleries Gardens without event. There was no indication of anyone following.

Seeing three taxis standing waiting for fares before they reached the Place de la Concorde, he got out, jumped into the first one, and told the driver to take him to the Gare d'Austerlitz. Now quite satisfied that he had lost his ex-colleagues he changed into another taxi, drove to the Gare de Lyon, collected the three paintings on offer from the left luggage locker and walked back to the Quai de Bercy at a comfortable pace.

To all outward appearance he was just an ordinary working man going about his lawful business with a tubular shaped parcel under his arm of a weight which caused him no difficulty. In fact, he had not been so tensed, so alert for days. In the comparative security of the taxi rides he had reviewed the events of the last hour with great care. One fact was now firmly established: The alarm bell had rung. At some point Gebler had recognized him. The key question had been answered beyond all doubt: It *is* me they are looking for. He was confident of his ability to play hide and seek with them for a little while longer; even the SSD were unlikely to be so gauche as to try to commit murder right out in the open here in Paris. But in a dark street? With a sniper's rifle? A bomb through the window of his hotel room? They had often done it before. That's what he would have done.

As he walked along the bank of the Seine, and waited for the traffic crossing the Pont de Bercy, there wasn't a nerve or a muscle in Horst's body that wasn't keyed for danger. He studied the entrances and exits of the grimy railway buildings, freight yards and warehouses and committed them to memory. He differentiated the cover provided by fixed and moveable objects in the parking lot. He judged

159

that the sidewalk near the river bank gave better visibility than that across the street, but also provided less cover. He noted where there was and was not a readily accessible pathway or track between the embankment wall and the water, and what the drop to it would be. He noted the maximum height of protection the wall gave against a shot fired from a moving boat. Above all he noted the people and gauged their movements. By the time he had gained the privacy of his hotel room, locked the door and moved a wardrobe against it, and from as far back in the room as possible studied the ugly view from the window overlooking the railway tracks, repair shops and signal boxes, Horst felt secure in the knowledge that he was once again alone in the world—for the moment, at any rate. But it was already a quarter to three, and it was starting to rain.

He took off his rough tweed coat, laid aside his tie and looked at himself in the mirror. Pity he had never thought that a total disguise would be necessary. It was too late now to rectify that, and until after he had received the cheque for the paintings and turned some of it into cash, it was too expensive. Wigs in particular, to fool anybody, need time and money, and he had neither to spare. He could at least change his general appearance; it wouldn't fool anyone for long, but every second's delay in recognition multiplies the chance of escape. He noticed the sky was darkening over and the rain was getting heavier. He took off his stained shirt, went over to the chipped wash basin and shaved off his beard. That unsightly bare half-inch patch above his right eye where the scar left by the stitches still showed clearly through a thin stubble of hair was like an advertisement. "Here I am, come and get me." He would have to have a hat; so long as the rain kept up it wouldn't be too conspicuous. What was the new image to be? He studied himself in the mirror again. He had lost weight these last two weeks. Small wonder. It made him look a bit gaunt, quite a bit older, he thought. No reason why the working fisherman from Bologna should not become a small-time businessman from Milan. Yes, that would suit Guiseppe Giancollo very well. There was nothing in an Italian passport which would belie it. He had one reasonably uncrumpled dark blue suit that might just pass. Cover it with a light raincoat—it would serve.

Horst put on his one clean white shirt, selected the best of the three ties he possessed, re-rolled the three paintings to be sold carefully in polythene sheeting and heavy brown paper, put the wardrobe back in its usual place, and went downstairs. He told the woman at the desk that he might be away for a day or two, but please keep the room for him, his plans were very uncertain. To reassure her, he offered to pay another three days rent now. *"C'est égal,"* she said pleasantly. So he didn't.

It was half past three as he opened the hotel door and the rain was getting heavier. The woman at the desk called out to him, "You'll need an umbrella."

"I haven't got one."

"Here," she called, "take this." He turned and walked back to her cluttered desk. "Someone left it here last week. People are always leaving umbrellas. Bring it back when you come."

He thanked her politely and walked out into the rain. The streets were nearly deserted now and, luckily, he did not have to wait long for a bus. His hawk eyes could detect no sign of suspicious activity in any direction. He had thrown them off his trail all right. But only for a little while. The meeting with Strassbourger was his only possible source of money. Rob a bank? Ridiculous. He had one bad-tempered government looking for him already. He didn't want another. For the first time it crossed his mind that he might be wanted for murder in Austria as well. That would make three. He had more urgent things to think about.

Wherever he arranged to meet Strassbourger they would be following. A railway station, a hotel lobby, a café, on a bus. They would be unlikely to kill him in a crowded place, but once on his trail again the safety catches would be off. And this time they would be expecting him. They would be better organized, and there would be more of them. Try the question the other way round: Was there anywhere it was reasonably certain they would not shoot him? Like in a police station maybe? And where he could have just a few seconds head start to try to lose them? There is one place in Paris where there are always a dozen gendarmes about—armed, alert, quick on the draw—and that place was no more than a few minutes walk from Strassbourger's.

What was going on at the Agence Maritime de la Mer Noire just off the Place de la Bastille was very much in line with the thoughts formulating in Horst Rheinberg's brain at that moment. Anna and the Head of Station, her ex-boss and good friend, Gregor Podgornov, may have been relaxing over the week-end, but they had seen to it that Klaus Bach and his men were kept busy. They were not particularly impressed with what Bach had to report that morning, and very much unimpressed when he returned in great excitement after the lunchtime excursions to report that they had positively identified the missing Rheinberg, only to lose him promptly again. Bach was sent away to call up all reinforcements and re-group them like a tight-meshed net round Leon Strassbourger. He was also instructed to keep on the air at all times. Three radio-equipped cars with well-armed drivers were ordered from an undercover Corsican organization which specialized in such services in return for exorbitant fees. Anna and Gregor remained in his office in endless discussion.

What Rheinberg was up to became increasingly obscure the more one tried to put together the few pieces they had to work with. There was no doubt in their minds that he had murdered the truck driver in Austria two weeks before—even for an SSD officer that required some explanation. His disappearance into Italy in a glider left them in no doubt that he had defected. But for what purpose? The attempt to sell paintings implied no more than an immediate need for money. In their reckoning, that could not be the whole story. On reflection, it didn't really matter. The order for his summary execution had been given and, in due course, would be carried out. If only those stupid Germans hadn't lost him!

"Sergeants!" Anna said with amused contempt.

Gregor knew the phrase well.

"Do you think he has defected to NATO and is playing some game with them as well?"

Anna raised her eyebrows in a mild gesture of surprise.

"To NATO?" she repeated. Then after a momentary pause, she continued. "I don't know." She paused a moment. "But I doubt it." For once in a very long time she instantly wondered if she had said a word too much? Her mind jumped to the thought of her friend at Ivry, and she resumed her customary sphinx-like countenance. Strange, after all these years, how a careless word at an unexpected moment might destroy something vital. At that moment Bach came through to say that Strassbourger had made a call at his bank on the way back to the store and was now working in his office. The first of the Corsican cars had arrived and was cruising on call in the Champs Élysée. He had a series of men under Gebler keeping close surveillance. There were five in the Boulevard des Capucines, five more in cars parked in the vicinity, and three in the alley that gave entrance to the Rue Edouard VII. No, none of his men were afraid of the rain, he replied angrily. His chief anxieties were traffic jams and the off chance that the police might pick up a strange traffic pattern operating intensively in the CB wavelengths. Both factors made the task difficult and neither could be eliminated. Two technicians, aided by a French Communist who worked in the Paris Telephone system, were still studying the problem of how to get a tap on Strassbourger's phone without being caught. There seemed to be a lot of gendarmes in the Boulevard des Capucines that afternoon. Anna listened to Bach's tale of woe with a certain cynical detachment.

The advance guards of the real storm were now sweeping down the eastern and southern slopes of Montmartre, and although it was not quite four o'clock, office and shop lights were on full all over Paris. Radio and TV weather forecasts were predicting that the worst of the North Sea storms driving across the Pas de Calais would hit the capital between six and seven this evening.

Horst stayed on the bus all the way to the Champs Élysées where, now feeling totally safe, he went into the foyer of a cinema and phoned Strassbourger. The art dealer seemed pleased to hear from him, thanked him for the lunch, and asked no questions. Yes, he had stopped off at his bank on the way back from lunch. He had the cheque in his pocket made out exactly as the signor had requested. Nothing he said, nor the way he said it, gave any hint of anxiety about anything that had happened at the restaurant, nor any awareness that he or anybody else was in some danger. For one horrible moment Horst wondered if Strassbourger himself was part of a manhunt team. There was nothing in those files, nothing in his behaviour, to support such a theory. Anyway, Horst had no doubts about his ability to deal with the sickly old man, provided he was alone with him. There was too much at stake to change course now. Strassbourger suddenly gave him an odd reassurance when he abruptly switched from Italian into French and started to address him as "Monsieur."

Horst interrupted, "Has that young man come into your office?"

The answer came back promptly, "Oui, monsieur," and Strassbourger carried on speaking as though nothing had happened. He would like a firm instruction from monsieur as soon as possible. Horst promised to phone back within the hour, and strode out into the storm.

He pulled the umbrella down closer over his bare head as the rain began to drive harder and the wind

165

to rise. He went into the first men's clothing store he found and bought a light-weight dark blue felt hat and a cheap raincoat, made in Taiwan "British style." With the clean white shirt, the respectably dull tie and a not too badly crumpled blue suit, he thought the whole ensemble could pass for a typical, modest style businessman from just about anywhere. At least from a distance of a few metres. The brim of the hat covered his bald spot comfortably without having to be pulled so far down it made him look like a cinema gangster.

He paid from his rapidly dwindling fund of cash and casually asked the store assistant if there were anywhere near here that he might rent a car. The man told him there was a garage up an alley three blocks away which he thought might be able to help him. They could. At a price. The charge was ninety-five francs an hour, three hours deposit in advance. Plus tax, of course. Horst bit his lip, and paid. The reserves were getting dangerously low, with little over for any unforeseen contingency. All the garage had available was a small red Renault. He drove it to the first car park he came to, got out and found a telephone kiosk. His watch showed a quarter to five. He called Strassbourger. Quickly, tersely, he gave him the minimum basic information he would need to make contact. At the rate traffic appeared to be moving all through the centre of the city Horst reckoned he would reach the rendezvous between fifteen and twenty minutes from now. The rain was, blessedly, easing off a little, at least for the moment.

Chapter 13

Horst drove up and down back streets, in and out of parking lots, until he was again satisfied that no one was following, and arrived outside the little Café du Presidence at the corner of Place Beauvau just as the clock struck five. Civil servants were pouring out of the Ministry of the Interior across the street, and police were guarding every door in sight. He drew up alongside the café, kept his engine running and his eyes glued to the rearview mirror. At three minutes after the hour he saw Strassbourger appear round the corner behind him and pulled slowly away from the curb. He did not wait to examine the various men who came round the corner next. He knew who they would be. He saw the art dealer suddenly quicken his pace and knew he had spotted the triangle of white paper placed in the Renault's rear window for identification. Just as he moved slowly into the Place Beauvau and approached the grand entrance of the Élysée Palace he saw the black van which had been moving at a leisurely speed a few yards behind Strassbourger suddenly accelerate. Had they spotted him already, or was it just coincidence? For once a kindly fate was watching over him. There were no less than four gendarmes frantically urging on the rush-hour traffic round the circle of Place Beauvau, and, better still, at least eight of the cars that swept out of the Rue Miromesnil immediately after him followed straight into the Faubourg St.-Honoré. The critical moment had arrived. Ignoring an angry squawk from the car immediately behind him, he moved right into the centre of the road, slowed down to a snail's pace, pulled his choke right out, and tapped his right foot on the accelerator so that the car stalled almost in the centre of President Giscard d'Estaing's gateway. As it came to a chugging, jerking stop no less than seven stalwart gendarmes were closing in on him, waving their batons and bellowing abuse. Two sentries literally leapt to the alert and held their rifles at the ready. Horst slipped the gearshift into low, turned the ignition key off, and made plaintive noises in Italian swinging his arms about in apparent despair and bewilderment. Within ten seconds the Rue Faubourg St.-Honoré behind him was a mass of jammed motor cars honking horns and irate policemen shouting, while that ahead of him was as clear as a race track very nearly all the way to the Rue Royale.

"Poussez!. Poussez!. Per. favori!" Horst was screaming at the top of his voice, while frantically grinding away at the starter and flicking the ignition key back to the off position every time it showed any sign of working. Then Strassbourger came alongside. Horst hurled the offside door open for him, screamed *"Poussez!"* louder than ever and the

little art dealer tumbled dripping wet into the seat beside him. Three burly heavyweights in blue were by now shoving the little car mightily. Horst pushed the choke back hard, put his foot on the clutch, and switched on the ignition. Within three seconds they hurtled off down an almost deserted street without a backward look. As he reached the Rue Royale one glance in the mirror assured him the nearest car was a good two blocks behind him, and the nearest tail must be at least five or six cars behind that. Missing a cursing taxi driver by a coat of paint, he turned north towards the Madeleine, through the market and on into Rue Tronchet. After that he took every second turning he came to, alternately right and left, and by the time he reached the Boulevard Haussmann he was as sure as anyone could be of anything that his pursuers had long since lost him again.

Strassbourger sat quite still and silent throughout all this performance. Horst had thought up a kind of explanation, but he was never asked for it. Perhaps his clients often do business this way, he thought. When he approached the Arc de Triomphe he turned into the comparative calm and open spaces of the Avenue Foch, reached into the back seat and handed his passenger the carefully packed roll containing the three paintings which formed the deal. To demonstrate his total good faith he also handed Strassbourger a pocket flashlight to assist his examination. He then turned south into the Rue de la Faisanderie and stopped the car exactly opposite the Police Station. The purchaser expressed himself satisfied with the merchandise and handed Horst an envelope. Horst opened it, took back the flashlight, and pronounced himself satisfied with the cheque for one hundred thousand francs made out precisely as he had specified. Without another word he started the car, drove back into the Avenue Foch, around the Arc de Triomphe a second time and turned right into the Avenue George V, finally stopping in front of the prestigious hotel grande luxe also named for that illustrious English monarch. The humble red Renault was well beneath the attention of the doormen of that grandiose establishment, so Strassbourger let himself out of the car. For the first time Horst noticed that his customer was showing signs of agitation, but neither of them said anything. The rain was coming down heavier again and in his anxiety to open his umbrella while carefully shielding the precious paintings, Strassbourger dropped the much needed implement onto the pavement. As he bent down to retrieve it a small leather wallet fell out of the raincoat pocket; neither of them noticed it. Strassbourger hurried for shelter into a waiting taxi and Horst drove off.

Leon Strassbourger's taxi pulled up outside 17 Boulevard des Capucines at ten minutes to six. He was thoroughly pleased with his pictures, had no worries about making a good and legitimate profit on the transaction, but he felt giddy, light-headed, and far from well. He understood the symptoms from long and painful experience. His state of increasing distress was not helped by the discovery that there had apparently been an accident directly in front of his store. Part of the road was barred off, a battered bicycle and a car with a smashed radiator were blocking traffic, and an ambulance with red beacons flashing stood at the curb. Police were everywhere. As he walked uneasily into the store he saw a group of people gathered round a man lying on a stretcher while two medical orderlies were busily administering first aid. Quite a crowd seemed to have assembled. One of two men quietly leaning against a tree at the fringe of the crowd saw him enter the store and hurriedly whispered something into a pocket radio. An instant later a large black sedan parked along the west side of the Madeleine flashed its headlights, three men materialized out of the shadows of the great church and walked towards it.

At almost exactly the same moment Rupert Conway was driving happily and unconcernedly up the Rue Royale to keep his six o'clock appointment with Strassbourger. His mind was solidly concentrated on Miss Schellenberg, Joseph Duveen and Andrea di Guisto, in that order. Seeing little chance of finding a parking space in the boulevard he drove round the east side of the church and pulled into the first empty spot he could find immediately behind it. He got out, locked both doors, and buttoning up his raincoat tight against the driving wind and rain, walked quickly towards the Boulevard des Capucines. At two minutes to six he walked calmly into the art dealer's store and one of the men under the tree spoke excitedly into his radio. Five men emerged from the black sedan by the Madeleine and fanned out along every possible route between there and the store. A minute later one of them signalled the man under the tree that he had just spotted a red Renault parked behind the church. At almost the same moment the men watching the front of Strassbourger's saw the last employees leave the store, the lights in the windows were switched off, and Strassbourger himself came and locked the door. The man with the radio spoke to his partner and the two of them faded a little farther back into the rain-sodden gloom. The medical orderlies at last began to move their patient into the waiting ambulance, the crowd dispersed, and police started to remove the traffic barriers.

Inside the store Rupert and Strassbourger were alone in the office. The conversation was relaxed and friendly, but Rupert was a little disturbed to find that the dealer was not. Rupert continued the casual American tourist approach and showed a genuine interest in the painting which was unrolled for his inspection. He was even pleasantly surprised by what he saw. Not a great painting, but well within the high standards Conway Vienna set itself. He would have preferred to buy it for rather less than forty thousand francs, but had little doubt of his ability to sell it for more. His only anxiety was the increasingly distressed behaviour of the man selling it to him. Such symptoms usually meant that there must be something phony going on, and he examined the canvas with even more than his usual care and thoroughness. Without undue conceit he worked on the theory, shared by nearly everyone who knew him, that if he couldn't find anything wrong with a picture then it must be right. Without making too much fuss he agreed to buy.

Rupert sat down at Strassbourger's desk to sign a stack of American Express travellers cheques and for the first time introduced the name of Duveen into the conversation. Strassbourger showed no noticeable reaction to the remark, but his agitation and distress about something was becoming every moment more obvious. He was shuffling about the office, going through his pockets, opening and shutting drawers. Twice he dropped small items on the floor and stumbled trying to pick them up. As Rupert finished signing the cheques Strassbourger dropped as though in exhaustion into a big arm chair opposite. He was shaking and sweat stood out on his forehead, but still he said nothing. Rupert had the strong impression his time was fast running out. He came straight to the real point.

"Did you ever do business with Lord Duveen?" he asked.

"Monsieur," came the halting reply, "you flatter me. If you were in the art business you would know very well that no painting the great Duveen handled would ever have been within my reach."

"Really? You surprise me," Rupert dissembled. Looking more closely at the man slumped in the chair across the desk he realized the stumbling words were perfectly sincere, but this man really was ill. His distress was not mental but physical, and whatever it was got visibly more serious every moment. Was he having a heart attack? God forbid! Not now! Rupert couldn't help feeling completely selfish about it. The only thing clear at the moment was that Leon Strassbourger showed every sign of passing out at any instant. Rupert took the Duveen letter out of his pocket and walked across to where the sick man was sitting hunched in his chair as though he had been hit in the stomach. There was no doubt about it now. Whatever was going on he had the dealer completely within his power— perhaps for only another few seconds. If he was ever to take direct action it must be now.

He held the letter right in front of the disabled man's face and said firmly, "This is your letter. I know you signed it. I want to know why." It was a demand, not a question.

Strassbourger stared squarely at the letter but his

face registered only pain and fear. Physical fear. He tried to speak, but at first the words were so slurred as to be almost unintelligible. For a moment it crossed Rupert's mind that he was drunk, but that didn't make sense. Then saliva began to trickle from the corners of his drooping mouth.

"Shhh . . . ugar," he gasped. "I bbb . . . eg you. I . . . I . . . I musht eat some . . . some . . . thing."

"God help us!" Rupert suddenly stumbled to it. "The man's diabetic," he cried out loud.

His mind flashed back and forth between the normal human desire to help someone in grave danger, and his fixed intention to achieve his own objective first. How much longer could Strassbourger last? There was no possible way of knowing. For a moment longer Rupert's hard-headed business judgement held him in its grip.

"Will you tell me about this letter?" The harshness of his own voice surprised him.

The stricken man in the chair stammered, gulped, his head fell forward on his chest. His lips quivered. But his eyes were still wide open, staring up at Rupert pathetically, like a wounded animal.

He struggled to form words. Rupert put his hand firmly under Strassbourger's chin, and lifted up his head. With a powerful effort he forced himself not to give way to all his natural, kindly impulses.

"Yesh . . . yesh . . . mon . . . shieur. I pp . . . promish. Oh God! Help me!" His head fell forward again. This time his eyes closed.

Rupert felt a flush of revulsion at his own actions. Quickly stuffing the signed cheques into the nearest envelope that came to hand, he jammed the envelope into Strassbourger's coat pocket, picked up his raincoat and threw it over the stricken man's shoulders, grabbed the plastic roll containing his purchase, and virtually dragged Strassbourger through the store and into the stormy street.

The rain and the wind were at their height. The ambulance had gone. The police had gone. There wasn't a uniform in sight. The lights in the shop windows gave no more than a soggy glow to pavements that had the appearance of rivers. Traffic had thinned to a trickle of moving vehicles fleeing the storm as fast as they dared and totally preoccupied with their own drivers' cares and anxieties. The foliage of the trees lining the boulevard was at its most luxuriant, the gale was tearing at them, hurtling leaves and blossoms and branches about like swarms of angry bees so that the watery light from the street lamps flickered like gun flashes. It was a good hundred metres to the nearest open café and nothing in between except a few hurrying figures of pedestrians, heads down, collars up, and beyond all hope of communication.

Rupert slammed the door of the art store behind them, secured Strassbourger's arm as best he could round his own shoulders, and grasping the man under the elbow with his other arm, slipping and stumbling through the torrents of water that flowed round them, struggled to propel the semiconscious form to the nearest point which held out any hope of human assistance. By ill luck Rupert had taken his charge on his right side, and his right leg was the bad one. They had not gone ten paces when he felt Strassbourger go completely limp, a dead weight. He had passed out cold, and Rupert's damaged right leg just wasn't up to it. He shifted his weight quickly to try prevent both of them falling heavily and as he lowered the unconscious man to the ground as gently as he could manage, a shot rang out! It was instantly followed by a splintering crash as the bullet hit the pavement a few inches in front of them and ricochetted into a shop window which splintered and crashed into the street. Then another shot. And another. Bullets were flying in all directions, glass was shattering and crashing onto the pavement, gun flashes were sparking from every doorway and from behind every tree and kiosk. Rupert thought he was back on the sodden slopes of Monte Cassino and the old army discipline instantly took charge. He lay absolutely still, his fingers digging into the pavement as though he could crawl under it for shelter from the hail of bullets going on round him. Another shot, this time very close behind him. He hadn't time to think where that one went when there was a loud scream and the unmistakable thud of a human body as it fell splashing into the street. Within a few seconds of the first shot powerful searchlights came on from both ends of the block, sirens began to blare, motor engines raced. The boulevard was alive with running men. The whole thing was over almost as suddenly as it had begun, except for a few more sporadic shots which seemed to be echoing up and down the Rue Edouard VII just opposite.

Lying frozen still on the sopping wet pavement Rupert had no idea what he had stumbled into. For a few seconds he really wasn't sure whether he was alive or dead. He felt the first real thrust of fear, the kind that jolts the adrenalin flow so you think you're going to faint, and numbs the brain with sheer helpless terror. The sound of running footsteps was surely coming straight at him and he was lying huddled, totally defenceless on the ground. He looked up and found himself staring straight into the barrel of an automatic grasped firmly in the strong competent hand of Jean-Paul Lucas.

"For God's sake, get him to a hospital," Rupert cried. "He's in a diabetic coma."

Chapter 14

Rupert and Lucas were a little late in reaching Quasimodo for dinner. "What a filthy night!" Rupert exclaimed genially as a waiter took his dripping mackintosh. Quasimodo has everything a civilized man could wish, but it is not for the tourists. Its patronage amongst lawyers, judges, senior civil servants and others who have their offices on the two historic islands in the Seine is such that it doesn't miss the tourists. It doesn't charge tourist prices either. Situated at the point of closest contact between the Ile St. Louis and the Ile de la Cité, its big plate-glass windows look directly across the adjoining bridge at the great buttressed eastern facade of Notre Dame Cathedral behind the high altar. Comfortably seated in the deeply upholstered green-velvet chairs in one corner of the window, Rupert and Lucas had a dramatic view of the huge gothic structure, its grotesque statuary flood-lit against the storm-blackened sky and framed by a baroque garland of evergreen plants and highly polished brass pots. The rain was now coming down so heavily that even Notre Dame's elaborate drainage system was overtaxed, and small cataracts were spurting into the air from the mouths and noses of every gargoyle.

Inside the cheerful hominess of the old restaurant, the bizarre, dream-like quality of the scene through the streaming window provided a phenomenal background for the enjoyment of the much needed and long overdue whiskies and Perrier. Johnny Walker Black Label with ice, but not too much, Rupert emphasized to the bar waiter. The evening had been eventful, all right, but not at all in the way he had anticipated. From his point of view it had not been notably successful. Although Strassbourger had declared his willingness to explain the Duveen letter, the coma had overcome him before he could start. Anyway, the prospects for such a confession now seemed reasonably certain, with the dealer safely tucked away in a private room at the Hôtel-Dieu under heavy police guard, and the doctor's assurance that the emergency treatment to restore insulin sufficiency should render him perfectly coherent again after a good night's rest.

Rupert and Lucas both ordered from the fixed price menu at fifty-six francs, a four-course ritual centring round one of Chef Pierre Nandon's specialties, *gibelotte de lapereau*. Rupert, being in no mood to concern himself about such dismal matters as economics, ordered a bottle of Vosne-Romanée 1961, and turned his attention to his guest.

"Now," he said decisively, "would you mind telling me what that was all about?"

Lucas raised his whiskey glass, said, "Santé," and smilingly obliged.

179

"I'll tell you what little I can. You know what Service Three is?"

"Deals with Communists."

"Subversives generally. And you've heard of Monsieur Guibaud?"

"Your boss. And Claude's."

"Correct. Well, last Friday afternoon an order emanating from the great man's desk instructed us that foreign agents, unspecifiied, were keeping close watch on Monsieur Strassbourger and that violence of some kind, unspecified, and against someone, unspecified, was anticipated. Not necessarily our business, but we don't particularly like foreign agents of any kind committing mayhem in France. Anyway, it offered us a unique opportunity to study such gentlemen on our own home ground, as you might say. Always interesting to see how other people operate. So, since then we have been carefully watching them watch Strassbourger. Can't say we're awfully impressed."

Whoever "they" were, that last remark coming from a senior French police officer did not surprise Rupert in the least.

"Who were they?" he asked.

"The one who was shot was carrying an official identification on him. Apparently, his name is Klaus Bach. He is an officer of the Secret Security Police of East Germany. When they get the bullet out of him and he's well enough to talk, it's going to be very interesting."

"I'm sure. What will you talk about?" Rupert enquired innocently.

Lucas allowed himself just the trace of a grin and said, "Charge of attempted murder to start with."

"It was he who fired that shot which just missed us?"

"There were a lot of shots that just missed you, but he fired the first one. Two of us saw it. His gun was lying where he fell. We have visual evidence, and ballistics. Open-and-shut case so far as he is concerned."

"You seem to have been remarkably well prepared for this little fracas this evening."

"As best we could," Lucas replied simply.

"Which means you must have been remarkably well informed."

"We like to think we are."

Lucas' style of speech was as closely clipped as his moustache and his straight black hair.

"You couldn't tell me how, naturally?"

Lucas chuckled. "Naturally. Because I honestly don't know. That's not my business. *Le Patron* tells me all I need to know. There is no secret about his interests; since the Palestinians obligingly moved their thugs out of Paris, studying the Russians has been his pet hobby horse."

"A remarkable man, *le Patron*."

"To his health, what's left of it!" Lucas raised his glass, sipped the ten-year-old Black Label with all the respect it deserved, and murmured, "Formidable!"

Rupert followed suit. "Tell me," he said, "something I haven't grasped at all. Why should these East German desperados want to kill poor little Strassbourger?"

Lucas set his glass back on the table, put his head on one side, and looked at Rupert quizzically. He was suddenly very serious.

"I didn't say they did," he replied. And after a

brief pause, "I thought you knew, my friend. That shot wasn't meant for Strassbourger . . . it was meant for you."

"They were trying to kill me!"

That appalling thought had never crossed Rupert's mind. He took two deep swallows of his drink and hailed the waiter to refill their glasses with somewhat less than his usual urbanity.

"But, whatever for? I know nothing about these goings-on. How could my little personal business with Strassbourger be of any interest to the East German boys?"

Lucas sighed softly to himself. He said, "Well, I don't suppose it was really. To the best of our knowledge they never heard of you either . . . but . . . you not only walked right into the middle of their game, for some inexplicable reason you and the man they were after took it into your heads to do a double act. I nearly had a stroke when I saw you turn up. *Le Patron* would have had my head on a plate if anything had happened to you, I can tell you."

Rupert's normally agile mind was in low gear battling uphill against the macabre idea that he had just escaped being murdered by the width of his coat collar. He looked at Lucas hard, but there was nothing in his manner to suggest he was trying to be funny.

"Sorry, old boy. I'm not following you. Meaning what?"

There was a pause while the waiter brought the *soupe á l'oignon* and carefully opened the bottle of rare classic Burgundy. Rupert gave both his deferential approval. Lucas put on his glasses and propped his note-book against the flower vase.

"According to the reports of my men, the sequence principal events was more or less as follows. At approximately four-fifty our friend Strassbourger walked out of his store, crossed the Place de la Madeleine into the Faubourg St.-Honoré, and a few minutes later disappeared into a red Renault outside the main gates of the Élysée Palace—driven by the man we knew was the one they wanted."

Rupert had by now recovered his *sang froid* but the mention of a red Renault sent another sudden rush of adrenalin to his head.

"We watched them attempt to follow that car. To be perfectly frank, we tried to follow it ourselves, but, as you well know, unlike television thrillers, in real life trying to follow a car in heavy traffic through a crowded city is virtually impossible nowadays. By a very clever little stratagem the driver eluded them. And us. By the way, he was wearing a dark blue felt hat and a light tan English raincoat. Got it?"

"I think I'm getting it. Go on."

"Well then. At five-fifty Strassbourger returned to his store, alone, from a taxi. As you saw, the place was surrounded by gendarmes. Then, at five fifty-two you parked a red Renault two blocks away—they had spotted that before you reached the store—and you walked right into the centre of the stage . . ."

Rupert finished the sentence, "Wearing a dark hat and a tan English raincoat."

"Exactly. You're about the same height and build, and in the dark and the rain it's not surprising they mistook you for him, really."

Rupert made a silent little prayer to his guardian angel and said, "And who in heaven's name is he?"

Lucas finished off the last of the *gibelotte*, washed it on its happy way with wine, wiped his mouth with the napkin, and then said, "That's something else you will have to ask *le Patron*. Probably a Communist defector of some kind. All I know is that he spoke Italian, and when the gentlemen tailing Strassbourger first spotted him earlier today they went berserk. My men very nearly had a shoot-out on their hands right outside the Hôtel de Ville."

Rupert sat contemplating the cataracts spouting from Notre Dame's gargoyles for a moment and then said pensively, "They must have wanted him pretty badly. This is all completely new to me. Lucky thing you chaps were there in force when I arrived. That traffic accident probably saved my life."

Lucas smiled grimly. "I can assure you, my friend, that was no accident. The victim will be back on duty first thing in the morning."

Rupert felt no urge to pursue the subject further, especially as *gâteau aux noix* was one of his particular favourites. They turned to other, less personal, subjects and enjoyed what remained of the dinner. As they were saying good-night Lucas remarked, "Better let me drive you home."

"Oh, don't bother. It's just round the corner."

"Yes, I know. Apartment 5, number 16. But let's play it safe if you don't mind."

"Oh no! God bless my soul, they're not still after me, are they?"

Lucas took his arm and gave him a reassuring grin.

"Not so far as we know. But I'd prefer to keep you in our sights until you leave Paris."

Rupert shuddered.

"Thanks very much, but I'd be grateful if you'd keep me almost anywhere except 'in your sights.' "

Lucas chuckled and a police sergeant opened the door to the car for them.

"I told you, if I let anything happen to you, *le Patron* would have my head on a plate. We'll look after you."

As they turned the corner into the Quai d'Anjou there was a sudden spluttering on the radio. Rupert's untrained ear only caught the occasional word, but Lucas looked happy. He said, "A note of congratulation from *le Patron*. He hopes you will come to his office at ten tomorrow morning."

"I'd be delighted."

As he entered the building and rang for the elevator Rupert noted three serious looking young men lurking in various corners of number 16. It didn't make him feel exactly hilarious, but on reflection, he found it comforting. As he started to undress he carefully unrolled his new purchase, laid it on the bed, and moved the reading lamp to reappraise it now it belonged to him. Quite pretty, he thought. And genuine; the brief provenance he and Strassbourger had had time to put together had undoubted integrity, his conscience was perfectly comfortable. The painting was by an obscure artist called Angelo Bargellini, about 1650. Not bad at forty thousand francs. Say, five thousand pounds? His Bond Street gallery should be able to get six for it. Maybe more. If Strassbourger came up trumps tomorrow, he might even keep it as a souvenir of this eventful evening.

It was too late to phone Miss Schellenberg so he went straight to bed, slept like a baby, and called her right after breakfast Tuesday morning. He did not tell her he still had no hard information at all bearing on their mutual puzzle; just that he would have the whole story available for her by this time tomorrow morning. The graces of the Connaught Hotel obviously had a relaxing effect on the formidable lady from Wisconsin. He found her much easier to talk to than when they had met in New York. She sounded positively interested. Although she gave him no indication what her final decision about disposal of the Andrea di Guisto might be, she called him "young man" only once. She promised to fly over to Paris first thing Wednesday morning, but said she must return to London before dinner. Rupert said he would get a car and meet her at the airport. Not the red Renault, he decided. Bobby Walker would want his most important client to be given the blue-ribbon treatment, he was sure. And be happy to pay for it.

Horst Rheinberg had driven away from the Hôtel George V, after dropping Strassbourger at five-thirty Monday evening, taken the first turning on to the Route Peripherique, swung over to the Auto-route de Normandie and driven half-way to Rouen. Just before seven o'clock the sign-post to Evreaux caught his attention, and as he was beginning to feel hungry, he turned off the highway and pulled into the first roadside inn he came to, where he ate a reasonably priced but thoroughly appetizing dinner. Then he drove leisurely back to Paris. He parked the car in the Boulevard Flandrin just off the western end of the Avenue Foch and left the key in the glove compartment. The police would be bound to find it within a very few hours and return it to its

186

rightful owner. He was careful to erase any possible fingerprints. He walked back to the Avenue Foch where he hailed a taxi and went to an all-night cinema in Montmartre where he promptly fell asleep to the accompaniment of some highly unlikely science fiction which seemed to concern mayhem, mass sex and vampires aboard a space ship somewhere off Mars.

He woke up just after six A.M. and walked the deserted streets to the nearest Metro from where he travelled to his little hotel off the Quai de Bercy. On the entire journey he detected nothing ominous nor unusual. The sleepy night porter handed him the key to his room without comment or reaction of any kind. The hallway and the stairs looked exactly as before, and the hair he had glued across the door jam three widths of his hand above the frayed carpet was precisely as he had left it yesterday afternoon. The quiet was broken only by an infrequent hooting of a train approaching the Gare de Lyon and its rattle over the points as it glided into the station.

By ten o'clock he was once again the respectable Italian businessman Guiseppe Giancollo from Milan, and presented himself in front of the window marked "Foreign Exchange" at the Banque Française et Italienne. He presented the banker's cheque made out to be cashed by them and waited patiently while they phoned the manager of Strassbourger's bank, as he knew they would. When the smiling clerk came back to assure him everything was in order he asked for five thousand francs in cash and the rest in American Express Travellers Cheques. He signed the numerous forms, thanked them politely, and walked down the street to the first travel agent's office he came to, where he was ushered into a small cubicle and soon joined by a charming young woman rejoicing in the title of a "Travel Coordinator." After an initial chat she went away to get airline and shipping schedules, and after a few minutes searching came up with the information that the Empressa Lineas Maritimas Argentinas had a combined passenger and freight ship sailing from Venice for Buenos Aires and Montevideo on Thursday. Three weeks complete rest at sea. How alluring! But, Venice? He knew the Red Brigade leaders there. From the train to the docks? Fifteen minutes, no more. What is it the French say? *Pas de problem*. A phone call to the firm's Paris agents yielded the welcome news that a few single cabins were still available. Arrangements were made for the necessary visas and a plane ticket to Trieste that same afternoon.

On the evening of the first of June Signor Guiseppe Giancollo with all his luggage, fifteen thousand U.S. dollars in American Express Travellers Cheques, and ample cash in his pocket sailed for the island of Guidecca, down the Grand Canal past the Doge's Palace and St. Mark's, out into the azure Adriatic. Horst Rheinberg was nothing but a memory which continued to agitate the KGB, the SSD and the Red Brigades.

Chapter 15

At three minutes to ten Tuesday morning Rupert arrived at the main entrance on the Quai des Orfèvres just as Claude Lebel was being helped from his modest official black Citröen. They exchanged warm greetings and Claude shifted the weight of his ailing old body from the chauffeur's strong arm onto Rupert's. The gendarmes on the door saluted Monsieur le Commissaire, which he really wasn't anymore, with their usual mixture of deference and friendliness, made the usual light-hearted remarks about having expected him to walk to the office this morning, and they went up in the elevator.

Half an hour later they came out again and were driven to the Hôtel-Dieu, where they were met by the house physician and Leon Strassbourger's family doctor who had been called in late last night when the patient's responses to the normal emergency treatment for diabetic coma had become erratic. For one ghastly moment Rupert thought he might be too late. To his intense relief the family doctor, a practical man, was reassuring.

"Monsieur Strassbourger has been my patient for many years," he explained. "He has been a diabetic since he was a very young man. It is remarkable he is still alive at all. With his medical history eventual deterioration of the kidneys is inevitable, I'm afraid, and it began to set in about a year ago. This complicates treatment and makes the course of an attack less predictable. I don't know what happened last evening, but he must have been very excited about something. At any rate, he forgot his milk and glucose at five o'clock, and then lost his syringe case, so when he felt the symptoms coming on there was nothing he could do in time to stave off the coma. It is a great blessing he was not alone, he could easily have collapsed and been dead before morning."

"He has recovered, I hope?" Rupert said with evident concern.

The doctor looked at him curiously, having no idea who he was, and replied, "Yes, he is quite all right now. Very weak, of course. I would like him to stay quiet here, for a day or two, under observation. There is always a risk of vascular degeneration after an attack like this."

The house physician informed the Monsieur le Commissaire politely but firmly that he could allow the patient to be questioned for half an hour only, and instructed them to try not to excite him. At any sign of distress they were to press the emergency button at the head of the bed. Lebel nodded his grizzled head and mumbled a promise that he would abide by the rule book. He had plenty of experience of hospitals. In return, and in the name of the Law, he must request total privacy. The doctors looked openly displeased but said nothing.

The room was in semi-darkness as Lebel and Rupert quietly entered, the blinds drawn just short of full length. The frail figure in the bed was lying propped up with pillows and apparently alert. As they closed the door behind them he spoke, "Good morning, gentlemen. How good of you to come to see me. Would you be so kind as to raise the blinds. I think we would want to see each other more clearly."

Rupert gladly did as he was asked as Claude Lebel shuffled himself into the nearest chair. Rupert turned back from the window and stood for a moment at the side of the bed in silence. Only one fact stood out in his mind at that moment. He had to learn the riddle of the Duveen letter, and he had to learn it within the next half-hour. Claude understood; the things he wanted to know could wait. Beyond that point, Rupert's thinking was in a turmoil. The events of the last twenty-four hours seemed so irrelevant to his own affairs, so unreal. He had been brave enough in his day, he hadn't won the Military Cross at Monte Cassino for nothing. But all this gun play and secret-agent scenario had been totally unexpected. The enigma of the shady art dealer was so different from the peaceful battle of wits for which he had prepared himself.

Now he was about to confront the critical moment in his own escapade without any clear plan of action at all. He was facing a man in his mid-sixties, obviously not far from death, who had spent most of his life struggling with an incurable disease, and whose life, so he had just been informed, he had been responsible for saving last night. He couldn't help feeling a little bit sorry for such a man. Until he thought about some of the items in that man's record: a traitor to his country in wartime who had betrayed his friends to the enemy; and a man who had for years used his particular knowledge and skills to conduct a highly dubious trade first with the Nazis and then with the Communists. Or so it appeared. What kind of a man was this who lay there looking so peaceful and welcoming?

"Please sit down." For all his ordeal, Strassbourger seemed to be entirely at ease. "I shall be happy to talk to you. I've long wanted to meet both of you."

That was not at all what either of them expected him to say. Rupert was amused to notice a flicker of surprise register on Lebel's normally inscrutable face. Strassbourger saw them exchange puzzled glances, and obviously enjoyed it.

"I had not expected Commissaire Lebel, but I recognized him the moment he came in. Years ago, when you were involved in various art fraud cases, monsieur, I always made a point of sitting in the public gallery at the Palais de Justice to listen to you give evidence. I learned a great deal from my experiences there."

Lebel grunted an incomprehensible acknowledgement of this dubious compliment.

"And you, Monsieur Conway," he put his hand out, lifted an envelope lying beside him on the bedside table, and dropped it back again. Rupert recognized it as the one containing the package of travellers cheques with which he had purchased the Bargellini last night.

"Once my brain started working this morning,

naturally the first thing I looked for were these. The signature, 'R. A. D. Conway,' intrigued me. I had taken you for an American, but I recalled you only referred to 'home.' You never gave me any clue to your identity. Then I remembered a photograph of you which appeared in *Weldkunst* a year or so ago. I knew then at once who you were. I'm flattered to have sold a painting to the great house of Conway Vienna."

The remark sounded perfectly genuine. Strassbourger continued, "I must also thank you. You saved my life last night."

It seemed he was conducting the interview. And producing all the surprises. Rupert actually blushed. He was edgy about the shortness of time and matters did not seem to show any sign of moving the way he wanted them to. He reached inside his coat pocket and took out the Duveen letter. Strassbourger indicated he understood the implication. He stretched out his hand and said, "May I see it, please?"

Rupert leaned across the bed and handed it to him. "You wrote that?" he said.

Without hesitation Strassbourger replied, "Yes, I wrote it. May I ask how it came into your hands after all these years?"

Rupert hurriedly outlined the circumstances surrounding his authentication of the Schellenberg collection.

"Oh, yes. I see," Strassbourger acknowledged simply. "More than twenty-five years ago. What an odd chance." He re-read the letter, his face a pale mask, registering nothing. If anything at all flashed across those weak, grey eyes the thick spectacles completely hid it.

Rupert watched a few more seconds slip irretrievably away.

"Monsieur Strassbourger. Time is too short for explanations, but, please, tell me the truth about this letter, the truth about the Andrea di Guisto."

The sick man looked up from the letter and a perfectly frank and open smile crossed his face. To Rupert's intense relief he said, "Yes, I would be happy to tell you. You may not believe it, but this"—he waved the fateful letter in the air—"is the only criminal action I have ever committed in my life."

Rupert said, "You will understand that Monsieur Lebel has a tape recorder."

"But of course," came the ready response. "If you would like to put the microphone on the bed, monsieur, please do."

Strassbourger began his story hesitantly, but without any trace of equivocation.

"I sold Mr. Schellenberg the Andrea di Guisto. It was my first really important sale. Atfer I came out of prison, you understand. It is not a fraud. It is perfectly genuine . . . probably the best thing di Guisto ever did."

Rupert interrupted, "I know that. But it seems to make that faked letter all the more unintelligible."

Strassbourger nodded. "At first sight, I accept that. But, not if you knew Mr. Schellenberg. You see, he was a strange man. I've not known any other self-made American multimillionaires, but if Hollywood movies get anywhere near the truth, he was a striking example. He wasn't a gracious, or cultured man. He was crude, ill-mannered. A blunt man, who talked mainly about money. Why he took to art collecting, I never knew. He knew nothing about

194

fine painting, and over the years I sold to him he never made any effort to find out. He wanted to own Italian Renaissance paintings, he never haggled over money, but he had to have bits of paper to prove they were real. In this case there was no paper . . . so, you see, I had to invent some."

Strassbourger's voice slowed to a stop. He closed his eyes, and there was an evident quiver of the shoulders. For one awful moment Rupert thought he was about to pass into another coma.

"You all right?" he said anxiously.

The drooping head lifted a little, the lips trembled, and Strassbourger said, "Yes, I'm all right. But the memory is not a happy one for me. I had to sell him the di Guisto." The voice had a completely new note. Almost of despair. "I had to. It was looted property, of course. We both knew Fritz must have stolen it, but it was all Heidi possessed. Only I could help her. I had to help her. I had to." His voice was pleading, but the ring was of total sincerity.

For the first time Lebel entered the discussion. He said softly, "Who is Heidi?"

The answer came in a whisper, "My sister." Having mentioned her name Strassbourger gave the appearance of having crossed his Rubicon. He gave himself a feeble shake, and pulled himself up a little straighter in the bed.

"Difficult to know just where to start," he said.

"Anywhere you like," Rupert said encouragingly. "Just so long as you can get it all in in twenty minutes."

"There were just two children, Heidi and me. She was two years younger. Being delicate from birth I never had many friends, couldn't mix like other

195

boys. We were happy enough in our home, our parents were good to us, but very soon we were aware they weren't very good to each other. The First World War really destroyed their marriage. The usual problem that afflicted so many families in Alsace those days—some became more and more French, others more and more German. Heidi and I just grew closer to each other. We built our own little world.

"When we were still very small father went off to Paris to seek his fortune. Mother always refused to go. We stayed at home, went to school there; only saw our father when he came home for holidays and passing visits. We loved him. When I finished at the Polytechnic I came to join him in the business. That was nineteen thirty-seven. The smell of war was already in the air, and I was by then diabetic, so there was no question of ever being able to do military service.

"That same year our mother died, and shortly after Heidi married Fritz Klaber. How Heidi got involved with a brute like Fritz I don't think even she ever knew. Silly schoolgirl passion, something like that. He was big and strong and handsome. That's about all she saw, I suppose. He was a Saarlander and a dedicated Nazi. Went straight from the Hitler Youth into the SS. Despite Heidi's pleadings he refused to be married in a church—went through one of those crazy tribal rituals Himmler devised for his men. Nothing about vows of love, or God's blessing or anything like that. Just the worship of Hitler and the fatherland and the fertility cult, with lots of strutting up and down waving banners and blowing trumpets. A kind of Wagnerian nightmare.

"Well, then the fighting started. Paris fell. France

surrendered, and the Nazis marched in. But the blackest day of all for our family was when Fritz was posted to Paris to work with the local Gestapo. Father and I knew from the day they arrived what hung over us. That broke his heart. Our first shock was the change in Heidi—we had not seen her for nearly two years, you understand. She was a broken woman, utterly miserable, but what could she do? The Nazis had a lot of special laws for the SS. For a wife to desert an officer was a criminal offence. Fritz himself had authority to send her to a concentration camp. He threatened her with it even when she pleaded for his consent to leave him. He used to enjoy talking about these things in front of father and me. He made a point of visiting us once a week—'our little family dinners' he called it. Always left his car and two SS guards standing outside the store. Before long we had little business, and no friends. No one would dare visit us any more."

Strassbourger started to cough and Rupert silently handed him a glass of water from the carafe on the table.

"Thank you," he murmured, and took a few sips, regathering his strength.

"So, somehow we lived on, like everyone else, through nineteen forty-one and forty-two. For me the fatal blow came that next winter; sometime in January nineteen forty-three, if I remember aright . . ."

The winter of 1942–43 was a hard one over the whole of Europe. The hardest in living memory. Shortage of all the amenities of life, but especially of food, was worst in the big cities, and worst of all in those capitals which shivered day and night under the brutal heel of the SS and the Gestapo. The war had started to go badly for Germany and the great landmark battle of Stalingrad lay only a few days in the future. As the disasters of Hitler's plans, and the failures of his messianic prophecies began relentlessly to mount, he responded with more and more insane cruelty. More and more of his finest soldiers, the cream of German manhood, found themselves ordered to stand and die a futile death rather than give up a few square metres of useless and indefensible rock or sand along the outer fringes of their conquests. Behind the battle fronts the louts and sadists of the SS and Gestapo who confined themselves to fighting nearly totally unarmed and defenceless civilians reacted against the slightest vestige of indiscipline or even suspicion with increasing savagery. By Hitler's explicit order every one of them down to the lowliest private had power to torture or kill at their personal discretion if they thought it "in the interests of the Reich." Throughout most of Europe the last traces of law and justice and civilization were swept away. It was a return to barbarism, and Hitler boasted of it.

In January 1943 food and fuel beyond the barest subsistence level were almost unobtainable for the ordinary citizen in Paris. Night after night the long-range bombers of the RAF and the USAF dropped their bombs on railways, bridges, factories and freight yards close to Paris, or flew over its environs on their way to drop them somewhere farther east.

On the night of January 28, 1943 Pierre Strassbourger, prematurely an old man, his hair pure white, his shaking arm and one side of his face showing the unmistakable ravages of at least one partial stroke, was sitting in his comfortably furnished but miserably cold sitting-room above the store in the Boulevard des Capucines, talking in low, faltering tones with his son, Leon. Besides being uncomfortably cold, the room was ill-lit. Under the latest decree issued from the office of "Ambassador" Otto Abetz to safeguard fuel supplies it was now *verboten* to use more than one light per room. So many of the comforts of life were *verboten* these days, and penalties for the smallest infringement depended solely on the whim of an investigating officer. As Lenin wrote, "the object of terror is to terrorize." The old man had himself prepared what little food his son had been able to buy, and the table was set for four people. There was even a bottle of wine, though they were reduced to drinking young, rough wine from Algeria, their own being unobtainable in the capital except for the Occupying Authorities and those to whom they chose to allocate it.

As if everyday conditions were not bad enough, January 28 was the occasion of the Strassbourger family's weekly descent into purgatory. They heard the sound of a powerful car draw up in the deserted street. That was a significant event in itself these days. There was the harsh bark of *"Yahwol, Herr Sturmbannfuhrer!"* Leon knew this was his cue to rush downstairs to open the door of the apartment. Fritz always got furious if he was kept waiting. Leon nervously opened the door at the bottom of the staircase, making sure no glimmer of light escaped into the street to offend the blackout regulations. Fritz pushed brusquely past Leon, who kissed Heidi tremulously, and they followed him up the stairs accompanied by an unending flow of abuse at the French from the brute in the black uniform.

Fritz, having most of the usual attributes of a natural bully, did not walk into a room, he marched. Once inside he clicked his heels as though his ancestors had been Prussian cavalrymen rather than Saarlander plumbers, threw his arm rigidly into the air, every finger muscle taut, and shouted "Heil Hitler!" Old Pierre was forced to the ultimate humiliation of being made to get painfully to his feet and mumble "Heil Hitler" in reply. If he did not, a torrent of abuse would descend upon his defenceless head, and what little chance there ever was of spending a reasonably civilized evening was blown apart before it started. Pierre's doctor had reluctantly advised him it was better to submit to the indignity than risk another stroke, though the moment was rapidly approaching when the dejected and enfeebled old art dealer would deliberately provoke such an attack and pray it might put a humane end to his miseries. What would then become of poor Leon he didn't allow himself to think. They were all trapped.

Fritz had brought a bottle of real cognac which he mostly drank to keep himself warm, though he graciously allowed his "family" a modest share. It helped to keep out some of the cold and, mercifully, dulled the sensibilities. Tonight his behaviour was, if anything, even more aggressive than ever. Despite the propaganda ravings, which were all the "news" Goebbels allowed European radio stations to broadcast, everyone listened to the BBC, and everyone in Paris knew that the German Army Group VI was on the verge of being totally surrounded by the Russians at Stalingrad. The inevitable reaction of Paris' slave-masters was to be even more bombastic and aggressive than usual. He complained and abused the shiftless French for the lack of food and light and heat, and in the same breath managed to boast that of course the best of everything must be reserved for the master race, the sons of the glorious Reich!

The meal was flavourful, but brief and miserable. When it was finished Fritz moved himself into the deepest arm chair in the room, demanded Heidi bring a stool for his feet, helped himself to another large draft of cognac and started hectoring the inoffensive and defenceless Leon.

"You have a friend, little Leon. One Gui Chamay," he announced loudly.

"Yes, we play chess together sometimes," Leon replied with his customary nervousness.

"Good," Fritz boomed. "I want you to play chess with Gui Chamay more often. You must become better friends."

Leon had no idea what this might be about. He shifted uneasily in his chair.

"I . . . I don't know what you mean," he stammered.

"I mean what I say," was the abrasive answer. "You are to see a great deal more of your friend Gui Chamay."

All Leon could think of to say was, "Why?"

The reply was virtually thrown across the room at him.

"Because your friend Gui Chamay is a fool! A criminal!"

Leon shuddered. "I . . . I can hardly believe it."

"What you believe is of no importance. I tell you it is so. And Gui Chamay has other friends. All fools. All criminals. They are involved in some stupid, treacherous group trying to smuggle British and

American air force men out of France. These are the murderers who nightly bomb our cities and kill our people. The Reich will not allow its enemies to escape." Fritz declaimed as though he were addressing a party rally at Nuremburg.

"I know nothing about such things," Leon blurted out.

"No? Don't you? Then you will find out, little brother. And when you find out you will tell me."

"But . . . I couldn't," Leon protested, trembling with fear.

"Oh, couldn't you?" Fritz reverted to his customary blustering, aggressive fortissimo. "The Gestapo think you could. You will say many stupid things to Gui Chamay. You will tell him that you, too, are a fool; that you want to help the British and the Yankee swine who kill our people. You will say you want to join Gui Chamay's group, and you will find out his other friends, and what they do. And each week when I come here you will tell me everything you find out."

Leon was terror-struck. Old Pierre gasped with horror. Heidi started to cry.

Leon stammered out, "But no! I couldn't do such a thing. Gui is my friend. I don't know anything about such matters. I couldn't. I couldn't!"

Fritz raised his voice another tone to its parade ground bark. "Oh yes you could, little brother. And I'll tell you exactly why you will." He heaved himself out of the deep chair and walked ponderously across the room to where Heidi was sitting slumped on an uncomfortable straight-backed chair. He put his hand possessively on her shoulder. She cringed.

"Yes, my Heidi. You know why your brother will do exactly as I tell him, don't you?"

Without releasing his grip on her shoulder, he turned to face the frightened Leon again.

"You would not like to see your sister sent to a concentration camp, would you, my little Leon?"

The way Fritz said it sounded as though he relished the prospect.

Old Pierre began to tremble and looked as though he might have another stroke on the spot. Reaching for the drop of cognac left in his glass his hand shook so much that most of the precious fluid dribbled down his shirt front. Leon was frozen with terror.

"Concentration camp!" Leon dug deep in his soul and found the strength to gasp, "Even you wouldn't do such a thing!"

"Of course I would!" Fritz was bellowing again. "The racial purity of those who serve the Greater Reich must be protected at all costs. We have risen above your decadent, bourgeois ideas, about love, and family; all the childish out-dated sentiments which have brought your precious Western democracies to destruction. It is only the State which matters! The glory of Hitler's Reich! My dear Heidi has committed a terrible crime." The harsh voice dropped to its ugliest, most threatening level. He looked down at the helpless, pathetic girl who cowered in front of him. "Haven't you, Heidi?"

Her sobbing became almost hysterical.

"Crime?" old Pierre stumbled over his words. "What crime has Heidi committed?"

"Hold your tongue, you old fool!" Fritz barked. "Perhaps we'll put you in a concentration camp too. Which would you prefer—Belsen, or Dachau maybe? You know Heidi's guilty secret."

The silence in the cold heavily shadowed room

was deathly. Fritz was enjoying every moment of it. It gave him just the kind of feeling of power he liked most; power over defenceless people.

Then he continued, "Your mother, old man, was a Jew. You knew that. Heidi married an officer of the SS without telling him she had Jewish blood. Under the laws of the Reich that is a high crime against the state. The Reichfurher SS has decreed the most severe penalties for such crime."

He paused again to savour the full effect of his tirade. Then he lowered his voice, and hissing like a snake, he added,

"But, in this case I think I might persuade the Gestapo to be lenient . . . if little Leon here does as I tell him."

Somehow the threatening, black mist slowly lifted. They were all back in the clean, bright hospital room again. It was 1979 after all.

Strassbourger lay back on his pillows exhausted by his ordeal.

"I swear to you, that is exactly how it happened. My father died a few days later. Fritz had killed him that night. Then, well, Fritz was posted to an SS unit in Italy and Heidi went back to their apartment in Nuremburg. I heard nothing of either of them again, for years. But the Paris Gestapo never took their knife out of me. I told them as little as I could. Twice they tortured me; of course, I told them. It was all bound to come out one day," he added, with the philosophic resignation of a man who knows his own death cannot be delayed much longer.

There was a long silence, and then Claude Lebel asked, "But why did you tell none of this at your trial?"

"What was the use? The charges against me were true. I offered to plead guilty, but my plea was disallowed. I didn't much care what happened to me at that time. Now, well, I am very near death anyway . . . I'm glad I had the chance to tell someone." His voice trailed off, and his hand fell limply onto the bed reminding Rupert sharply that, interesting though all this was, he still had nothing positive relating to the Duveen letter.

"But Heidi's painting? The di Guisto?" he said rather more forcefully than he had intended.

Strassbourger looked up and smiled apologetically.

"Of course. I'm sorry. It played such a small part in my memories. It was all quite simple really. You know I was released from prison in nineteen fifty-three. Somehow or other Heidi heard that Strassbourger's shop had reopened, and she came here. I had thought she was dead—most of Nuremburg was bombed flat, as you know. She told me that Fritz had returned from Italy soon after the end of the war. He had acquired false papers of course, the usual thing. The only possession he brought with him was the di Guisto. Neither Heidi nor I ever talked about it, but of course we both knew he must have looted it from somewhere. Justice very quickly caught up with him; the American Zone authorities tracked him down and arrested him. She told me he was charged with shooting some British prisoners-of-war in Italy. Just the sort of thing he would have done. They hanged him. Heidi had nothing. Her health was too broken to work. She was sick, desperate, in need of money, and all she had was the painting. She stayed with me for a few weeks and then, one day, Mr. Schellenberg came into my store for the first time. He said he wanted to buy Renaissance paintings. I had very little stock at that time, so I showed him Heidi's di Guisto, and he liked it. He said he wanted it but would not buy it without some provenance to support its authenticity. I had to bluff, said I could find something. Of course there was nothing, and I couldn't go to any public authority on a painting I knew to be stolen. So, I made it up. Duveen's was the best name I could think of to impress him. He paid me fifty thousand old francs for it. Not much nowadays, but it was sufficient for Heidi's purpose."

"Which was?" Rupert asked.

"She did the usual thing for those days. Went to South America and became a nun."

"Where is she now?"

"She died many years ago," he said with resignation. "In a leper colony. In Paraguay."

The half-hour was more than up, and the patient clearly worn out by the exertions of dragging up so much unhappiness from the depths of his memory. The house physician appeared in the doorway bristling with signs that the visitors had outstayed their welcome as far as he was concerned. Rupert stood for a moment looking down at the care-worn face on the bed. Strassbourger took his thick glasses off and rubbed his eyes. He had aged years in the last twenty-four hours. He looked like a man who knew his last days could not now be very far ahead of him, but somehow or other, the tension had gone. Rupert thought that for the first time since he had met him, Leon Strassbourger had a strange air of contentment—as though he had at last come to terms with a fate that had never been kind to him.

Waving away the evident irritation of the house

physician with a gesture of the left hand, Lebel tottered to his feet and leaned against the foot of the bed for support.

He said, "Just two final brief points, Monsieur Strassbourger. I accept your explanation of your connection with the Nazis; but, in recent years we find you somehow much involved with the Communist regime of East Germany. That is . . . ah . . . how should I put it . . . a rather unpleasant coincidence, is it not?"

Strassbourger replied wearily, "I know what you mean. It does not put me in a pretty light, does it? But, coincidence? No, it was no coincidence. You know, Monsieur Commissaire, better than I do, most of the men who set up the East German security and espionage organizations are old Nazis. They just changed their uniforms and went to work for the Russians. They continued to use me whenever it suited them. I suppose I'm a coward, but they were always ready with threats. The young man with the pinched face, Louis, is only the latest in a long line of contact men they planted on me. If I fire him, they will just do something more unpleasant."

Lebel made a note, and nodded. "And last, monsieur. Who was the man in the red car?"

The answer came direct and without hesitation. "I honestly don't know. He never gave me a name, and I've long learned it is a waste of time asking a man in that situation. He can make up anything he likes. He just came in off the street two weeks ago and offered me three very good pictures. Monsieur Conway now owns one of them."

That was something else Rupert had not known. "No idea where he came from?"

"Italy, I presumed. He spoke perfect Italian."

As they turned to leave before the house physician became violent, Rupert turned to the man in the bed and extended his hand. "Thank you," he said quietly.

Strassbourger took it in his feeble grasp, smiled and murmured, "I'm proud to have sold a painting to you."

Claude insisted that as they were on his home ground it was to be his lunch. He told the police chauffeur to drive to Le Vert Galant at the grander other end of the Ile de la Cité facing the vast courtyard in front of the Palais de Justice. Le Vert Galant presents the real *haute cuisine française* but still remains discretely out of range of all but the most discerning tourists.

Rupert had now completed his mission. He knew all he had set out to discover, and Claude had it carefully stored away on his tape for Miss Schellenberg's education and edification. There was little left to be said about Strassbourger. "A rogue, of course. Probably has plenty on his conscience. But not vicious. Can't help feeling sorry for the fella, really."

Claude grunted, "Naturally."

But there were many missing pieces Rupert longed to explore. The anonymous Italian picture seller; his relationship with the Communist gunmen; all this was terra incognita. How much would Claude tell him? He placed too high a value on their friendship, had too much respect for his friend's brain to ask any question to which Claude's duty forbade an answer. To try to approach that inscrutable intelligence, whose most famous quality was discretion, with the object of trying to trip it would not only be stupid, it would be insulting.

The waiter set down before them two huge servings of Vert Galant's bouillabaisse and departed. As Claude tucked his napkin carefully under his chin, Rupert asked, "Claude, can you tell me, who was the man in the red car?"

The old detective slurped away happily, wiped his drooping moustache and grunted, "As Strassbourger said, he came from Italy. Spoke Italian."

"Yes," Rupert replied good-humouredly. "So do I. And English, French and German."

Claude looked up from the outsize china bowl, tilted one eyebrow, and picked a small fish bone from between his teeth with the wide-eyed innocence of a schoolboy.

"No reason why you shouldn't know. He was German, East. A defector of some kind. Quite an important one, according to my information."

Rupert might have guessed that from what Lucas had told him last night, but at least this was positive.

"Do you know his name?"

"Rheinberg," Claude said directly. "Horst Rheinberg. A policeman. That's all we have on our records at present."

There was a pause while the waiter set down a large platter of cheeses, with seven different kinds of breads and biscuits, all so artistically decorated with fresh fruit that it might have been the model for a still life by some great Dutch artist of the sixteenth century.

Rupert began again, "Was it really just chance they mistook me for him?"

"We have no reason to think anything different."

"What an extraordinary coincidence."

"Extraordinary? Huh. A murderous coincidence."

As they were saying good-bye outside the restaurant, Rupert could not resist one last overwhelming piece of curiosity.

"I don't suppose you could tell me, but this murderous coincidence as you called it . . . it nearly cost me my life. It would have if you had not been so remarkably well-informed about what the East Germans were doing. Just how was that?"

The old man looked intently into Rupert's dark blue eyes, and shook his head humourously.

"Ah," he said. "You Anglo-Saxons. Will you never learn? We French have always been closer to the Russians than you have. Do you not know there are still quite a number of people of French birth living in Russia? Some of them in very influential positions."

Chapter 16

At five minutes after ten Wednesday morning Miss Schellenberg, looking positively radiant and almost radiating good will, stepped out of an Air France flight from London and into the limousine Rupert had hired for the occasion. She was immaculate in black as usual, complete with pearls and the handsome diamond solitaire. She had a small suitcase and a parcel she carried herself.

As they drove into the city Rupert briefly explained all he had learned yesterday about the di Guisto. She seemed a little puzzled as to just how Claude Lebel had got into the act, but Rupert said nothing beyond the fact that they were old friends. She even deigned to be visibly impressed by the respect with which they were received at the Quai des Orfèvres, while Rupert found confidence in the thought that Claude would be a match even for this formidable female. At least she would find difficulty challenging his authority concerning the strange story she was about to hear.

They made themselves comfortable in Claude's office on the sixth floor, the tape was placed on the desk and they all sat in total silence while it was played through. When it was finished Rupert was determined to say nothing, to try, if possible, to make her play the first card. But she was a doughty adversary. She sat silent for the best part of a minute until Rupert and Claude both decided to force her hand by solemnly occupying themselves with loading their pipes. Almost in self-defence she finally said, "Very interesting."

Rupert's impatience got the better of him. Waving out the match and puffing hard, he said directly, "Are you convinced?"

She looked him straight in the face, and without any indication of feeling one way or the other, she said, "Yes, I'm convinced."

At least she hadn't called him "young man" which was encouraging. After another long pause she said, "What do you want me to do?"

Rupert struggled to suppress a sigh of relief and replied with equal directness, "Let me give it back to the nuns of San Leonardo."

The words were hardly out of his mouth when he knew he had put it badly. There was a flash of that vibrant electricity from deep down behind her eyes somewhere and she said firmly, "No. I won't do that." Rupert clenched his teeth and realized perfectly well she saw him do it.

Without the slightest change of expression she continued, "That is a pleasure I intend to enjoy myself." Then she literally beamed at him, "But, if you would care to accompany me . . . as my guest, of course."

Rupert made no attempt to suppress this sigh. He

had always been sure there was a heart of gold somewhere beneath that granite facade.

Claude looked at his watch and, noticing it was nearly twelve o'clock, said, "I think it is time for a little *aperitif*."

There was a momentary glimmer of the old, stern-faced Miss Schellenberg, and she ventured a mild, "I don't approve of drinking alcohol in the morning."

Claude showed no emotion at all as he sighed and said, "Alas, dear lady, that is sad. But this is my office, and I do."

The old tiger's courage still never failed him. She even joined them, sipping an amontillado with all the graces of a Madrileno donna.

Rupert took her to lunch at the Ritz and felt relaxed in her presence for the first time. For the first time she addressed him as "Rupert" instead of "young man," and the next time he called her "Miss Schellenberg" she said in her accustomed voice of authority, "In the future you call me Mary."

They discussed the timing of the visit to the Tyrol.

"Why not tomorrow?" Mary suggested.

"That's why you brought a suitcase with you!"

She exhibited a slightly guilty smile.

"I guess I really made my mind up back in New York. But I told Bobby Walker not to tell you."

"What about your appointment in Chicago?"

"Those confounded lawyers can wait another day or two. They've kept me waiting for years."

Over coffee Rupert asked, "One thing I don't understand. Just why are you so impatient to sell the collection? Do you really want to part with such beautiful things?"

She laughed. "Oh yes. I can bear it all right. I

know what you've been thinking about me—I have more money than is good for any woman already. Yes, I have. But Walter's collection has never brought pleasure to anybody since the day he started it. It didn't even bring him any pleasure. It was just something he felt he had to do because other millionaires did it. In the seven years since he died they've brought me nothing but trouble. I've fought for my rights, and now that I've proved my point, I'm tired of the whole business. Anyway, our little hick town doesn't need an art gallery. What it needs is a new hospital, and I intend to see they get it."

On Thursday morning Rupert Conway and Mary Schellenberg flew off to Milan where she had hired a chauffeur-driven car to take them to San Leonardo di Monte. The only bad moment of the journey was when she thought the Italian customs might search her luggage. She was damned if she was going to pay customs duty for the privilege of giving that painting back to the nuns.

As they were boarding the plane for Italy, the KGB contingent gathered in the Aeroflot VIP lounge at Charles de Gaulle Airport received another nasty shock. Departure time for the Moscow flight came and went and Anna did not show up to occupy her scheduled seat. Despite frantic weeks of searching they never found trace of her again. She lives in a small town in France these days where she teaches. And her name isn't Anna anymore. She had had enough excitement for one lifetime, and her friend in Ivry fixed everything very comfortably for her. After all, they owed it to her; she was probably the most successful double agent France has had since the war.

After languishing for seven months in Vincennes prison Klaus Bach was exchanged for three unsuspecting French travellers who were found somewhere east of Berlin with a camera they should not have been carrying and were arrested as spies. But Bach was no help to anybody else.

Rupert finally got back to Vienna on Saturday afternoon, where he and Sandra and Charlie drove straight down to the country house at Semmering. It had been a hunting lodge belonging to grandfather Eisenbath and Rupert had spent some of his happiest boyhood holidays there in the company of his brother George, whose life had been so suddenly and so tragically ended in a tank attack with the Welsh Guards during the last North African campaign. Like all Jewish-owned property in Austria the Semmering house had been confiscated by the Nazis and left in a state of sad disrepair at the end of the war. It had taken him years to recover the property and restore it. It was his favourite retreat, with its tall pine forests, its superb view down the valley of the Murz to Kapfenburg and the Styrian Alps, and its happy memories. 5B Stephensplatz was his own creation but the house at Semmering was "family"; its owners and creators had been Sandra's grandparents too. He really tried, and often succeeded, in feeling that they shared a kind of brother-and-sister relationship here.

Since there was no Evangelischekirke nearer than Vienna, they drove over to the little Catholic church the other side of the village to Sunday morning ser-

vice. His Welsh grandfather, a staunch chapel-going
Methodist, would have had a fit, but to Rupert a
church was a church; at that moment he had a lot to
thank his Creator for and didn't believe the Almighty cared very much where he went to do it. Besides, Rupert had a particular liking for Father Jo-
hann and was a staunch supporter of his boys club.
He thought the reverend father talked a good deal
of sense from his pulpit that morning.

They were just settling themselves into deep easy
chairs on the stone-flagged terrace overlooking the
river some five hundred feet below, and Rupert had
just opened a well-chilled bottle of Bollinger 1966,
another vital part of his Sunday ritual, when, to
Sandra's undisguised disgust, they heard the phone
ring. A moment later Anna Erhoffer, who kept
house for Rupert while her husband tended the
neighbouring woods belonging to a member of the
Habsburg family, announced that the Herr Hofrat
Liebmann wished to speak to the Herr Doktor.

"Oh damn Jo Liebmann." Sandra was provoked.

Rupert smiled a big brotherly admonishment and
went inside.

He was gone nearly five minutes while Sandra's
mind circled round the problem of when she was
ever going to get him to relax for more than a few
hours consecutively. She was just reaching the point
where she was beginning to think, "I suppose I'll
have to marry the brute," when he returned.

He filled both their glasses, took his usual time
filling his blessed pipe, and sat down in pensive silence:

Sandra said, "So silent? What tidings was big Jo
bearing?"

216

Rupert furrowed his brows and scratched his nose.

"What a strange world we live in," he mused.

Sandra waited patiently.

"You remember the case of the vanishing murderer? The man who killed the truck driver up on the Brenner last month, and then disappeared into Italy?"

"Supposed to be some kind of East German policeman, wasn't he?"

"That was the theory. Well they've found him at last."

"Really? Where?"

"The *carabinieri* found his body washed up on the south coast of Sicily on Friday night. With a bullet through his brain. For some extraordinary reason, the Red Brigade in Venice have claimed responsibility." He gazed at the distant mountains for a moment, and then said, "I wonder if that was the man in the red car in Paris?"

More Best-selling
Espionage and Suspense
from Pinnacle Books